Also By Camille Mariani

Lucille's Lie
Aletha's Will
Pandora's Hope
Links To Death
Prelude To Murder
Invitation To Die
Astrid's Place
Abram's Puzzle

AURA
OF PERIL

Camille Mariani

iUniverse, Inc.
Bloomington

Aura Of Peril

This is a work of fiction. All of the characters, names, incidents, organizations, and dialogue in this novel are either the products of the author's imagination or are used fictitiously.

iUniverse books may be ordered through booksellers or by contacting:

iUniverse
1663 Liberty Drive
Bloomington, IN 47403
www.iuniverse.com
1-800-Authors (1-800-288-4677)

Because of the dynamic nature of the Internet, any web addresses or links contained in this book may have changed since publication and may no longer be valid. The views expressed in this work are solely those of the author and do not necessarily reflect the views of the publisher, and the publisher hereby disclaims any responsibility for them.

Any people depicted in stock imagery provided by Thinkstock are models, and such images are being used for illustrative purposes only.

Certain stock imagery © Thinkstock.

ISBN: 978-1-4759-8822-2 (sc)
ISBN: 978-1-4759-8823-9 (e)

Printed in the United States of America.

iUniverse rev. date: 4/30/2013

To Aileen Vincent-Barwood: colleague first; friend always.

Intolerance has been the curse of every age and state.
--Samuel Davies

You cannot depend on your eyes when
your imagination is out of focus.
--Mark Twain

CHAPTER 1

Later Abram would say the ring's curse was nothing but a superstitious wives tale, that he lived in the real world, not influenced by fakery or voodoo. Lives couldn't be affected by a long-ago curse perpetuated through a century of creative story-tellers sitting around a fire in the dark of night, adding to an already ridiculous fabrication. He would say he never believed it, not for a second.

(Which would be a lie, of course.)

. . . .

Gunnar came to Fairchance on Thursday, four days before his sister's wedding scheduled for New Year's Day, 1990. Not only would he discuss his role as best man and take part in the church rehearsal, but he planned to give Abram a very special ring. Gunnar himself had a wedding ceremony three years ago, held at the in-laws' home. He placed on Charlotte's finger a heart-engraved gold band to match the diamond engagement ring she had chosen. She preferred new, expensive things and would not want an old ring, no matter how much family history it represented. She had faults, but being sentimental was not one of them. For that reason

Gunnar never showed her the ring nor did he tell her the story behind it.

"You're going out?" Gunnar asked when his sister came down the stairs and into the living room to say she was off.

"Ya." Astrid said. "I'm going to a funeral. Our chief of police died. It wasn't unexpected, but he will be missed. Helluva good guy. See you in a couple of hours."

"Take care," Abram said.

"She's in a hurry," Gunnar said after she left.

"Like always. She rushes off to work or to a dental appointment as if there wasn't a minute to spare, even if she's early."

"Guess you've become pretty well acquainted, living here together."

Abram observed the male version of Astrid, a bit shorter, blue eyes, silky blond hair like hers--the man who would soon be his brother-in-law. In the past few weeks he'd grown to understand Gunnar's directness, much like Astrid's.

"We pretty well understand each other. She's fun, easy to tease. She's usually sensible. I've learned enough about her to know that she's a good woman."

"She is that. Never thought much about her, myself, especially never thought of her getting married. To me, she was just my older sister, without a lot of frills. She was better than me at just about everything, and I never won a fight with her when we were kids."

After some moments of contemplation, Gunnar said, "You make a good couple."

Abram laughed. "I hope so. I never took her on in hand-to-hand combat, though. I have an idea I'd lose, too. She's strong. Her imagination sometimes runs away with her."

He discovered her vivid imagination when she wanted a handy-man to make renovations to the Sears model house she had just

2

bought. He met her at the front door, and she took him through the house, outlining what she expected him to do. It forewarned a certain unrealistic expectation, but she could not be dissuaded back then, before the house was blown up by her crazy neighbor. She envisioned possibilities beyond Abram's grasp, and that took a strong imagination. Now she appeared to be focused on building a new house, but with the same basic lines as the original one. He could build it, and he would, though why she was hung up on that design, he didn't know.

"I remember that," Gunnar said. "When we were growing up she thought up more games and pranks. They usually got us in trouble."

Gunnar settled back in the recliner, and considered this grand house that Astrid had rented. He studied the intricate carving in the marble fireplace mantelpiece, comparing its elegance to the plain stone fireplace at his farm. He no longer felt envious of Astrid over the wealth their grandfather had left her. He had finally settled down to farm work, thankful for the productive agricultural business that was his inheritance. He now had plans to hire more hands, and had figured out how to operate the sprawling farm more efficiently, first by expanding the already lucrative milk products franchise, Axelgren Farms. He no longer searched for an escape to an easier life. He now believed that his inheritance was actually more valuable than his sister's hefty share of the money. It had taken Astrid herself, sitting with him one afternoon, outlining just what he needed to do in order to reach this point of optimism. She was a good farm manager, better than he was; however, she chose not to pursue the idea of buying a farm but to remain with the newspaper.

For a few minutes the two men reached back in their minds for more to say on the subject of Astrid. Abram, however, could think only of her caring heart, how she had brought him through the painful days following surgery to repair his torn rotator cuff. Then she fussed over him after his close shave with death following entombment, all the while forgetting about the horror of her own escape from the hands of killers intent on grabbing her money and doing away with her. He had every reason to love her without reservation.

At last, Gunnar broke the silence.

"Just wondering, Abram. You have a ring for the wedding ceremony?"

Abram's breath escaped slowly. This was something he'd been putting off and he knew it was probably too late to do anything about it.

"No. You know that I haven't had a full-time job for months. But with this part-time job at the Sheriff's Office, I now have a bit of money set aside. Funny thing. Astrid hasn't said a word about it. I told her I can wear an old ring my brother had. Good enough for me. Before this day's end, though, I need to go to the pawn shop and see if I can find one for her. I don't know why I've been putting it off, but..."

"No, no, my friend. That's not good enough at all. Look, I brought a ring with me, and before you say anything, let me tell you about it."

Abram could feel the warmth in his face. This was embarrassing, having to consider a gift from Astrid's brother, especially a wedding ring. Obviously that was what Gunnar had in mind. Thoughts of how to refuse it with civility ran through his mind, all the way from just plain "No thanks" to placing the decision at Astrid's feet. He liked Gunnar, and wanted to remain friends, especially now that they were to be brothers-in-law.

"I don't know," he said.

"Of course you don't, but like I said, let me explain. Okay?"

"I guess."

Gunnar took a black velvet box from his jacket pocket and opened it for Abram to see. "Oh, wow," was exactly the response he expected, though he was sure Abram didn't know what he was looking at. Later he would describe the gems as he had learned from a jeweler, the gold band with five emerald-cut Burmese sapphires encased on each side by bead set diamonds. Flashing like a city's winking night lights, it appeared to be new.

"Pretty, huh? There's just one flaw with it."

"It doesn't show."

"No. It isn't anything you can see. This is an heirloom, handed down to my grandfather by his mother, who gave him a word of warning. She insisted that the ring was cursed and that anyone who wore it would be ill fated. Therefore, she had never worn it."

To Abram, curses on persons, animals, things were too ridiculous.

"A ring that's cursed? It doesn't look like the Hope diamond."

"Well, in my view, there's no such thing as a curse on it, or anything else for that matter. I would have put it on my wife's finger, but she's not impressed with antiques. I doubt the curse would have frightened her, but she wants everything new. I'm not saying she's hard to live with for that reason, only that she's expensive. Anyway, now that she's expecting…"

"Expecting? I didn't know that. Hey. Congratulations, man."

Gunnar put on that aw-shucks grin that prospective fathers get.

"It's made a difference in both of us. She keeps busy making baby things, and I'm beginning to see our bank balance rise, at least for now that she's not out shopping every Saturday. I meant to tell Astrid and you both at the same time. Oh well. I'll tell her when she gets home. For now, about the ring."

He laid the open box on the coffee table for display.

"The story goes that my great, great Aunt Alva got it from her husband, and, at the age of 25, she died while she was trying to pull it off her finger. Why was she taking it off? Who knows? Maybe the ring was too tight and hurt her finger, maybe she was mad at her husband and wanted to fling it at him. Why she died is another unanswered question. I think she must have had some fatal sickness, maybe cancer or a heart problem that they didn't know much about and couldn't cure back then."

He stopped to take a cookie off the plate that Astrid had set out for them before leaving.

"Mmm. These are good. Chocolate chip. My favorite. Want one?"

Abram had eaten his share just before Gunnar arrived, so he shook his head. His curiosity was rising.

"How did the ring get such a bad reputation? Was that the only reason?"

"No. Alva had a married sister and they all lived together in a big house in Stockholm, Sweden. After Alva died, the sister took the ring off Alva's finger, so the story goes, and put it on her own finger. She was admiring it as she walked toward the staircase, missed the top step and fell down the long flight. Just before she drew her last breath, she looked up at my great, great-grandfather, and said, 'This ring is cursed.' He didn't believe such nonsense and passed the ring on to his son, my great-grandfather, who then presented it to his bride. Her first baby was stillborn, and she died giving birth to her second child, my grandfather. So before he came to the United States, his father gave him the ring and told him about the curse."

Intrigued, Abram blurted, "What happened to your grand-mother?"

"She died young, but not from wearing the ring. She had pneumonia. Farfar…"

"Wait a minute. Farfar?"

"That's Swedish for grandfather. I heard the word when I was a young kid and called my grandfather Farfar ever since."

Abram tried unsuccessfully to suppress a smile at the foreign word. Gunnar stiffened in pretense of being offended.

"I'll say it different, then, for your untrained ear. *Grandfather* had not given the ring to his bride. Instead, he put it away in a box where he kept important papers. Many years later, when he became sick, Astrid was just out of college and working in New York State. Grandfather had me get that box and take it to him so he could show me the ring. He told me the story of the curse and advised me to keep it and sell it if I ever had financial trouble. Of course, it was then that he also told me about the will he'd drawn up. Astrid didn't know this. When it became apparent that Grandfather was in his last days, she returned and stayed by his side all through the rest of his illness. And she never saw or heard about the ring."

"So she doesn't know about the curse? What would she say if she found out?"

"She might be upset since she *is* a bit superstitious, as you probably know by now." Abram nodded. "If you want to take a chance that the curse is just hogwash, it's yours to put on her finger. I'll never say a word, and you wouldn't need to, either."

"How can I possibly keep it from her? I mean, she knows I'm poor as a church mouse. I couldn't buy something this valuable at a pawn shop."

"I guess you could say it's an heirloom from a great aunt. You wouldn't have to say that it was *her* relative. It wouldn't actually be lying. You'd just not be giving her the full story."

Abram thought for a long time. It was a beautiful ring. He could surprise her with it Monday at the ceremony. It would sound credible that he just didn't tell her about this ring, only about his brother's ring for himself. He probably could get away with it. What could be the worst to happen? She'd eventually learn the truth, have a brief moment of anger, but get over it. Sure. What harm could there be in that?

"All right," he said. "I'll accept it. Maybe someday I can pay you for it."

Gunnar knew the ring's value, and he laughed. It would take Abram years to pay for it at the rate he was making money.

"Never," Gunnar said. "I don't want or need it. You take it with my blessing."

Abram picked up the little box and lightly touched the gems. If Astrid liked it as much as he did, she'd be happy enough to wear it. However, he had just one more fleeting thought.

What if the ring really is cursed?

CHAPTER 2

Astrid and Abram would never forget the significance of January 1, 1990, the day they were married in the Fairchance First Baptist Church. Their schedule allowed for a brief appearance at the reception, return home for luggage and change of clothes, drive to the Bangor International Airport, and flight to Florida for a three-week honeymoon, including a Caribbean cruise.

"I hope the Jeep won't be snowed in when we return," Astrid said, after Abram parked in the outdoor long-term parking area at the airport. "They're predicting snow."

"I wouldn't be surprised to find it buried. In the meantime, we'll just forget it and enjoy sunshine and warmth, good food, and a great cruise."

"Among other things," Astrid said.

Abram hesitated as he reached for the suitcases, pulled her closer and found willing lips for his kiss. He whispered, "Oh yeah, among other things."

They had taken time at home to consummate the marriage. "After all," Abram said then, "it will be several hours before we retire again." They almost forgot about the flight.

Inside the airport, they checked in, and learned that boarding would be in an hour. They rode on the escalator to the upper level, walked across the blue carpet to the snack shop where they bought sandwiches and coffee, sat across from each other at a table, and ignored the other patrons. Astrid divided her attention between Abram and the ring, while he viewed his wife with pride. But the ring troubled him. Her astonishment when he placed it on her finger at the ceremony had been perfect. At the time, he felt elated to give her the gem-studded ring, but his conscience kept nagging that it wasn't really his to give, that she ought to know it was her own family heirloom. Still, he couldn't bring himself to admit it, even when she asked how he obtained such a lovely ring.

"Oh, it's a hand-me-down. A great, great-aunt originally owned it."

"And you've kept it after all you've been through. It's gorgeous. I love it."

He'd known greater guilt trips than the one he had right then, but it was hard to remember when.

The boarding announcement came through the loudspeakers.

"We'd better take the rest of lunch with us," he said. "Need to board now."

It appeared that everyone in Maine was headed for the Sunshine State. When the plane was ready for take-off, all seats were occupied.

They watched the demonstration of unlikely methods to survive a crash or emergency landing, while Astrid pulled out her tray, and laid her hands on it in order to continue her study of the elegant stones.

"Abram, I went on a cruise once and the ship had very nice shops where you could purchase things at a discount, especially on the final day at sea. I think we could find you a new ring that would match mine better, since yours is silver instead of gold. Do you agree?"

"If that's what you want, it's okay with me."

"Isn't it amazing that the ring fits me as if it had been sized to my finger?"

"Amazing. You know…"

"Know what?" she asked when he didn't continue.

He had almost told her the truth, but couldn't disappoint her now. It probably wasn't so amazing that the ring fit well, considering that the Swedish ancestor probably had the same general finger features, long and slender.

"Oh, I was just going to say that if you want a less showy ring, we could find a pair to match."

"No. I love this ring. I'll never part with it."

She left her hand on the tray but gazed out the window as they reached an altitude high above the clouds. The sun shone into the cabin. Rather than pull down her shade, Astrid let its rays bounce off the stones in dazzling display.

"I can't believe you had it all the time that you were in such financial difficulty. A lot of men would have hawked it."

"Yeah, well I didn't exactly have it."

"Oh? You mean your brother had it? Did he leave it to you?"

"You could say that."

After all, Gunnar was his brother now, sort of. So he wasn't really lying, just not completing the explanation, just as Gunnar had said he should do. Of course, it was possible that his brother-in-law could be wrong. It might have been better to talk it over with Astrid right up front. There was a big possibility that she would have gone along with wearing the ring, and Abram wouldn't have this bilious feeling every time she brought up how much she loved the ring.

Abram recalled Gunnar's words: *She was admiring it as she walked toward the staircase, missed the top step, and fell down the long flight.*

11

A sudden side-to-side movement shot terror through Abram. The plane dropped. They were on their way to a fiery death! That ring…but wait; no, the pilot was announcing "turbulence ahead." From the queasy feeling in his stomach, Abram knew he already had turbulence. He made himself relax and looked around to see if anyone had noticed that he likely left a hand impression in each seat arm. Astrid had not yet taken her eyes off the ring.

"Don't you think you've admired the ring long enough, Dear? Don't want to draw attention to it now, do we?"

He'd never seen Astrid so taken with a piece of jewelry. In fact, he wasn't sure she had any jewelry, so this was an unexpected turn of events, and not too welcome. He'd thought the suggestion of matching rings would please her. Instead, she brushed it off, not with disdain, but with another hand flourish and smile as if the ring were a kitten. If it had come from his own great, great-aunt, it wouldn't bother him, but it was from hers. And it had a curse. Not that he believed it for a second.

Still, the whole thing--the ring, the story behind it, deceiving Astrid--made him edgy. How long could he carry on this façade?

****

When she came to Florida with college friends so many years ago, it was hot and humid, so walking out of the Tampa International Airport into what felt like a cold winter day back home, Astrid regretted having chosen a sleeveless blouse to wear. Worse yet, her sweater was in her suitcase.

"I thought Florida was sunny and hot," Abram said, in that casual, almost indifferent tone that could upset Astrid's equilibrium because she knew that he really meant it was damned uncomfortable and probably all her fault.

"Ya. It was hot when I was here before," Astrid said, trying to sound unfazed.

"When was that, Sweetheart? In August?"

Ignoring the remark, she said, "I'll go over to the window and inquire about our limo. You wait with the luggage."

"Yes, sir," Abram said with a salute.

He could be so aggravating.

"You know what?" she said. "I'm going to take my carry-on to the ladies' room and put on something warmer. I'll be right back."

"Okay. I'll be here."

She saw the signs for rest rooms and headed down a hallway toward the right one, when a man jumped out in front of her from the men's room. Not only was he exposed, but he was wagging his exposure at her as well.

She gave him a shove that sent him against the men's room swinging door and said, "Zip it up, Bozo."

She was too cold to put up with this sort of action. If he should pursue her, she'd make him sorry he didn't do as she said. Obviously, he was too drugged to know what world he was in. She should report the incident, but figured he'd be arrested soon enough. She couldn't be bothered.

When she came out, the man was gone, and she hurried back to the street where, to her surprise, Abram appeared perfectly at ease as the crowd around him jostled and pushed each other, some hailing taxis, others running for waiting cars, and everyone seemingly indifferent to traffic officers' whistles as they directed the endless stream of vehicles and persons. Astrid, on the other hand, hated this confusion. They had started out at a calm, well-ordered airport in Bangor, rushed across a busy depot in Philadelphia for their next plane, and landed in Tampa tired, hungry, and now very cold, only to find an uncaring, non-apologetic mass of humanity that Astrid didn't want to be around for long.

She waved at Abram and went to the line of passengers waiting for information at the sidewalk window. She took up the rear and looked at the vehicles by the curb. All at once she saw her name on a card held high by a man dressed in black, like a chauffeur, only less formal, leaning against his limo, a blue Mercury Grand Marquis. Having the voice to reach Abram, she yelled, "Abram. Over here. Our ride is here."

To the driver, she said, "I'll go over and help him with the luggage. Wait a minute."

"I'll he'p you, ma'am. My name's Travis."

"Thanks, Travis. I'm Astrid and my husband is Abram."

From his quick frown, Astrid wondered if it might be improper for the hotel workers to call guests by their first names. Travis tipped his cap at Abram, picked up two large bags, leaving the carry-ons to his fares, and led the way back to the limo trunk, where he packed it all neatly.

Astrid ran her hand over the blue velvet back seat. "Nice," she whispered. They were soon riding past both tall and low buildings, nightclubs, auto dealerships, eateries, banks, shops. Astrid caught sight of a sign announcing I-75 South, and they joined a stream of vehicles, many passing them along a four-lane highway. On the other side of the median, another four lanes accommodated as many cars and trucks heading north.

"Busy route," she said. "Is it always this busy, Travis?"

"Nevah seen it different, jes worse when somethin' special's goin' on."

"How could it be worse?"

"You'd be surprised. Get a crack-up, and you can be waitin' to get by it for hours."

"Not good if you need to catch a plane."

She sat back, put her arm through Abram's and laid her head on his shoulder. In three weeks they would be among those going north on the other side, but for now they were on their way to a beautiful motel where they could relax, go swimming, catch up on sleep (or not), read the newspapers, watch TV, shop, sightsee. Next week, they would be on a peaceful eastern Caribbean cruise, with ports of call where they would soak up the sun and watch boats and swimmers in the turquoise sea. That was how the cruise brochures pictured the adventure and that's just how Astrid knew it would be--absolutely heavenly.

CHAPTER 3

They signed in at the front desk, took the key to room 232, and climbed the stairs to the second floor after being told their luggage would be right up. Abram unlocked the door, and gave Astrid a longing look, while clinging to his just barely healed shoulder.

"As much as I'd love to carry you over the threshold…"

"Dammit, Abram. Don't be a fool."

She brushed past him and walked over a red carpet to the picture window for a look at the ocean view, which the brochure had described as "fantastic."

"What's this?" Astrid craned her head from one side to the other. "Do you see water anywhere, Abram? All I can see is a white building and shrubbery."

"Oh, no, not a problem already."

At her side, he also could not see water. Then he made a closer examination of the room.

"Water isn't all that's missing, I'd say."

"Huh?" Astrid turned around and saw the unmade twin beds, one with a missing pillow, an ashtray full of cigarette butts. A wine or coffee stain covered a large part of the carpet between the beds.

Astrid sniffed the rancid air. They looked at each other just as the porter rapped on the door.

Astrid strode over to it and stood directly in front of the young man.

"You can take the bags back to the lobby. We're not staying here," she said, in full voice.

The porter looked horrified.

"Yes, ma'am. Y'all don't like the room?"

"We-all certainly do not like the room. Come on, Abram. We'll find something else."

He did not reply, but followed as Astrid got into the service elevator with the porter. It was a quick ride down, quick and silent except for Astrid's heavy breathing. When the elevator settled to a stop and the door opened, she went to the front desk and let her words fly.

"We will not be staying here. That room is disgraceful. I doubt that the beds are cold yet. What rating is this hotel? X?"

The pretty young desk clerk raised her eyebrows in an indifferent pose, but her face did turn a shade pink, nearly the shade of her hair.

"What can we do to make it better?"

"You can burn it, for all I give a damn. Here's your key." She dug in her bag until she found what she wanted. "And your brochure. You really ought to think of having a new one printed. It should read, 'No view, no class, but plenty of filth. Just what no honeymooners want.' Besides that, even if all the rest were okay, we asked for a queen bed, not twins. Here's a tip for the porter. I paid more than enough for anything else, including the *limousine* ride. Now. Where's a telephone and directory of nearby hotels and motels?"

The clerk looked as if she would argue, but only for a minute, until her color returned to normal.

"There's a public telephone just outside on the right. Here's a brochure on the area accommodations."

Before she could unleash more venom, Astrid felt herself being pulled gently backward. Abram stepped forward, and his voice roared like a hungry bear's in springtime.

"We're not going outside to make a call. We're on our honeymoon, and I'm in no mood to search for a decent bed tonight. I expect you will provide limo service to wherever we want to go. In the meantime, we'll consider whether to report this dump to the Better Business Bureau, for starters. If we don't get our deposit back, we'll get the sheriff to look over the operation. But I doubt that you have any shady business going on. Right? What could the law possibly find wrong in this honeymoon haven?"

He waved a hand in the direction of the resident lobby loungers, a collection of languishing humanity, mostly women, and the scene increased his already explosive anger. Slouched in grungy pink chairs, wearing skirts that looked more like short slips than outer clothing, four females focused spiritless eyes on him as they variously applied more layers of lipstick and streaks of eye shadow, readying for their night romps like the vampires he imagined they were.

Astrid watched this man, her husband, who threatened to bring down the law on the place. Was this Abram Lincoln, the mild-mannered, always calm, peaceful-to-a-fault man she'd married? Astrid stood back and studied him with interest while he handled the situation. Slamming his hand on the counter, his jaw taut and his eyes narrowed, Abram leaned forward as if he might jump over the barrier and attack the young woman if she didn't act. He pointed to the switchboard.

"You able to make calls from there?"

Now the clerk resembled a white geisha doll. She nodded.

"Don't worry, sir. We'll see that you are transported. Let me make a call or two for you." A nervous laugh, then, "We don't want you to go away unhappy."

Three telephone calls later, she flashed a weak smile and said, "This is high season here, of course, and most all hotels and motels are fully occupied. But I found a very nice place with a view of the Gulf, and a queen bed. I think you will be happy there. It's the Sunset Breeze Hotel. They have a pool."

Abram ignored her coy look and reached for Astrid's left hand, leading her outside. His grip was so firm that the wedding ring dug into her flesh. She said nothing. If ever there was a time to exercise silence, this would be it. His forcefulness caught her by surprise, almost like seeing him for the first time. No one could doubt his positive qualities, but this assertive side, as commanding as any army sergeant, had not surfaced before, not like this. The bad start to their honeymoon would undoubtedly turn into the best of honeymoons after all.

****

Dee watched lazy, heavy snowflakes drift to earth and knew she couldn't wait much longer or she wouldn't get her car out of the parking lot. Now she wished she hadn't traded her SUV for a four-door Chevy, but the salesman was just too persuasive and she ended up driving off the lot in a shiny new black sedan.

"I don't think she's coming," Dee said. "It's beginning to look rough out there. You want to go along, Charlie, while you can still get through?"

She had given the editor's chair to Charlie when he joined *The Bugle* staff last week, during the quiet days of Christmas season. For now she hadn't changed anything in the office since she took over as publisher. Coping with the volume of work proved to be more challenging than she had expected now that Astrid and Abram were married and on a long honeymoon, and Natalie had given up the editor's post to go with her doctor husband and family to North Carolina. With the three of them—Natalie, Dee, and Astrid—the newspaper hadn't lacked for local news. Astrid was so capable when she arrived half a year ago that she soon moved into general reporting in addition to her primary function as sports editor. Now it was up to Dee to decide whether to hire a reporter. If she herself worked in the publisher's office upstairs rather than to serve as editor/publisher and work here in the editorial room, she would need another reporter. It was a decision that she hadn't yet made, and for now her old friend from Twin Ports, Charlie Hart, would fill in as editor and she would simply continue in her old reporter capacity. Her desk faced and abutted Natalie's, now Charlie's, at the front of the converted old Cape, overlooking Fairchance Main Street.

"She probably didn't dare drive in this snowstorm," Dee said. "Can't really blame her, but I'd like to get a few interviews done so we can choose someone soon. I really think I don't want a dual role here."

"How many have applied?"

"Two. I interviewed a guy just out of high school. No work experience, and if his speech is any indication, no language skill, either. I think he's trying to prove to his parents that he can work without a college education. I say that because he said he had just returned from Florida where he'd been for the past month. I asked if he was working there, and he said no, just being a beach bum. Takes money for that kind of life."

"You bet it does. Do you know his family at all?"

"No. But he said they're both teachers, which may explain his rebellious feeling about education."

Charlie wiped frosty fog from his window to look again at the falling snow.

"Main Street's a mess. I hope they get the plows out soon. Lucky that Astrid and Abram got away yesterday."

"I haven't heard if flights are canceled today. Too bad you couldn't have been at the wedding yesterday, Charlie. I was sorry to leave you alone, even for an hour. Astrid looked so beautiful. You seldom see her gussied up and sparkling. I'm happy for her. I think Abram's a good man."

"From what I've seen of Astrid, I'm sure she would have only a good man," he said. "You know, I think I'll call Jen and tell her I'll stay at the motel for the night. I don't take chances on the road any more, not since I totaled my car a few years back."

"You did? Jenny never told me. Were you hurt?"

"Naw, not hurt. But shaken up enough so that I've been cautious ever since."

Dee studied the application she had received from the next interviewee.

"This woman coming in is Cathryn, if she comes. I won't wait much longer, myself."

"What did you say her last name is?" Charlie asked.

"Cotter. She signed the letter Cat Cotter. Now that's a name for you. I talked with her by phone. She has a very high-pitched..."

Before she could finish the sentence, a wisp of a woman whose nose was bright red from the cold wind, rushed through the door, bundled for arctic weather in brown plaid wool head scarf, long brown wool coat sporting a wet and matted fur collar, hand-knit brown mittens, and heavy boots mostly hidden by the coat. Dee guessed her age to be around 68 or 70, though her hazel eyes suggested a young spirit.

"Hello," she said in a high but firm voice. "I'm Cat Cotter, here for my interview."

She removed the head scarf revealing hair, as white as the snow she shook from the covering.

Dee had no age prejudice, but it crossed her mind that this Cathryn, or Cat, wouldn't be physically up to the sometimes hectic pace of the office.

"Whom do I talk with?"

The woman's diction was clear, her grammar obviously correct. Dee stood and walked toward her.

"Thank you for coming in such bad weather, Mrs. Cotter."

Cathryn took off a mitten and gripped the hand held out to her. If Dee expected a dishrag handshake, she was mistaken.

"Come, sit over here. Shall I call you Mrs. Cotter or Cathryn or Cat?"

"Employers generally call their workers by first names. Call me Cat," She turned to Charlie. "And this is?"

"This is Charlie Hart. He's acting editor, at least until I decide what the arrangements will be in the newsroom."

"Very well. I would have been here earlier, but the walking is difficult, so much snow."

"How far did you walk?"

"I live on Maple Street."

"Maple Street! That's where the school is. You walked all that way in this snowstorm?"

"I did. If I had known how fast the snow was piling up, I would have started sooner. I allowed for my usual walking time of 15 minutes, but it took me ten minutes longer."

Dee shook her head, speechless. To walk through heavy snow would be tiring even for her, and Maple Street was a mile from here. It could have strained her heart.

"Do you always walk, Cat?" She wasn't sure she liked that name. "You don't drive?"

"I drive. My husband has the car today. He had a doctor's appointment in Bangor and hasn't returned yet."

Charlie picked up on that.

22

"And you're not worried that he might not get through?"

"He'll get through. A little snow won't stop him. If he gets stuck, he'll shovel himself out."

"But he…that is, at his age, is it wise to shovel heavy snow?"

"His age? Now listen to me. Young people think anyone over 65 is old and ready to take to a wheelchair. We're both 72, and there haven't been more than a half dozen times in our 50 years of marriage that we've missed our Saturday night sex. And we intend to keep it that way. I have my eyesight, my hearing, and my good sense. I take no pills, my blood pressure is normal, my heart is strong. As for doing this job, I taught high school English grammar for 25 years, and for the five years my husband worked in Boston, I was a reporter for the *Christian Science Monitor*. I sent you clippings of my work along with my resume."

"Yes," Dee said. "I was impressed with your work. How long has it been since you worked there?"

"Just one year. We never did give up our home here. Roy finally decided he wanted to retire and return to Maine, so he could finish a book of poetry and sketches he has been outlining for years. He'll publish in about a year. In the meantime, I am at loose ends without work to do--outside employment, that is--and I don't care to deal with young men and women in high school any longer. At the senior level, they know a great deal more than they'll ever know again."

The end of Cat's straight nose appeared to be two halves glued together. She sniffed, flaring both slender nostrils when she finished talking.

Dee smiled at what she said and at how the woman had no doubt that she could do whatever she wanted to do.

"I'm still interviewing candidates," she said. "I expect that I'll make a decision next week. In the meantime, Charlie is about to leave."

Dee looked across at him. "You'll take Cathryn…Cat… home, Charlie?"

"Of course I will. Be glad to."

He pushed back his chair. But Cat didn't rise from hers.

"You have so many candidates to interview that you can't make a decision now? I did walk in heavy, wet snow to get here. I would have thought you had time enough to read my resume and clippings, enough time to make up your mind already."

Sheepish guilt flooded over Dee. It was true she had decided that because Cat was an excellent writer she would hire her. That was before she met this old woman with pure white hair. Her immediate reaction was to reject her out of hand, to wait for a younger person to come along, one who could go where the news was--a fire, an accident, a high school pageant. Could she cover an evening meeting of city council or school board members? Would she be able to take photos? There were so many stories to cover, and sometimes even the young reporters became exhausted by the time the newspaper was put to bed.

But it was wrong to judge her on age alone. The woman was a bit of the school marm authority type. Could she soften her manner if she needed to gain the confidence of an aloof person who didn't really want to open up to a reporter?

Well, there was one way to find out.

"We've just finished with this week's newspaper and are ready to get out of here ourselves. Tell you what, Cat. You come here tomorrow if the roads are clear at about one o'clock, and I'll assign a couple of interviews and you can come in next Monday to write them up. If all goes to my satisfaction, you'll have the job. But conversely, you understand, if for some reason I think that you and the job aren't compatible, I will let you know that I can't use you. Satisfactory?"

"Satisfactory. You'll see. Older people are not useless. Now, my man, shall we go?"

Cat bundled up again while Charlie retrieved his coat from the closet. He opened the door for her to leave first, hesitated, looked back at Dee and raised an eyebrow. His shrug said it all.

CHAPTER 4

Astrid decided to wait for Abram in the lounge where she could see some activity both in the hotel as well as well as on the street. It had been several years since she lived in a large city. She didn't like Tampa when they arrived, but here everything moved at a much slower pace, without much traffic on this resort street so that walking around should not be a problem. In fact she was surprised not to see more pedestrians. Likely this area was not of particular interest for shopping, and the beach was behind the hotel, with few bathers braving the cold air. Like everyone else, Abram and Astrid weren't interested in the water view and swimming, either.

They had been at the Sunset Breeze Hotel for two full days and hadn't yet gone out to sightsee or shop. The weather, they were told by the housekeeper, was still quite cold, but warmer than the day they arrived at the airport. In the course of clean-up yesterday, she had told them of a nearby shopping mall with boutiques, restaurants, a theater, hairstylists, barber shops. Today Astrid suggested that they go see this place and maybe swim in the pool after lunch.

Now she was getting fidgety and tired of reading *Newsweek*. She picked up a week-old newspaper from the bottom shelf of her chairside table and saw that it had a summary of 1989 events. She started to read about Ronald Reagan's farewell address, the Soviet Union's withdrawal from Afghanistan which ended nine years of fighting there, the $13million bounty that Ayatollah Khomaini placed on Salman Rushdie's head as author of *The Satanic Verses*. The hotel played soft music, and Astrid listened to Bette Midler's *Wind Beneath My Wings*, as only she could sing it.

She looked at the two men in the center of the hotel lounge, sitting one on each side of a square table, and wearing heavy jackets. Odd positions to take for playing chess. In all the games she had played, she had faced the opposition and paid undivided attention to the board, a great deal more than these two did. These two faced the street, looked down at the board only occasionally and moved a piece quickly. They seemed far more interested in something out in the street, visible through the wide windows.

She stood up, hung her bag over her shoulder and casually walked around, first glancing at brochures on a table beside the elevators, then wandering behind the two men where she stopped, glanced down at the board. They were only pretending to play. Obviously they didn't know how to play the game, not with the king set aside as if it had been captured. She raised her eyes to see what they were watching so intently. The long row of buildings, like everything around the area, had been upgraded for the new/old appearance that this resort area apparently required. Straight across the street was a red brick bank. Two white columns flanked a pair of wood doors with intricately carved designs. A square window on the left with Old English lettering said Bank.

So what were these would-be chess players up to? What had them so interested? Traffic on the street was sparse. In front of the bank was a white car, parallel-parked. A woman tottered along the sidewalk and entered the dress shop at left. At right of the bank, a dog walker coaxed two overly groomed poodles along. A white-haired man on shaky legs bent over a cane to exit the bank.

As if on signal, the two chess players bolted from their chairs, slammed through the double glass doors, and ran across the street just after another white car pulled up, parked, and two men emerged from the front seat. One handed each man a long-barrel gun, the other had a briefcase almost the size of a carry-on, and they all quickly disappeared inside the bank.

Now she understood.

"Someone call the police," Astrid yelled at the desk clerk, who looked up in surprise. "Don't wait, there's a robbery going on across the street at the bank. Hurry. Call the police."

Abram was just getting off the elevator when he heard the last words.

"Call the police? What is it? What's happened?"

Astrid beckoned for him to join her at the window.

"Over there. Four men just went into that bank. They all had weapons. We should do something."

"What do you suggest? Run over and say, 'Here we are, you can shoot us now?' I think we'll stay put."

She pushed him aside and scooted to the desk.

"Did you call the police?"

"They're on their way. That bank was hit three weeks ago."

"Oh God. Nice neighborhood."

She went back to the window, where she paced back and forth, straining to see the robbers when they came out of the bank. It seemed like 15 minutes before they came out with that big briefcase that Astrid presumed was now full of money.

"There they are. Where are the police?" She looked over at the seemingly unconcerned black-eyed beauty behind the desk. "You sure you called the police?"

"They'll be here."

After the two white cars sped off, police sirens whined and spinning blue lights came into view from the opposite direction. Astrid felt sick and light-headed.

"Why are they so late?" she yelled, noting the desk clerk's wide-open eyes. "If they'd been here just minutes ago, they'd have caught those guys."

She headed for the front doors and pushed through while Abram yelled behind her, "Where do you think you're going, Astrid?"

"I'm gonna tell the police what I saw. I can describe two of the men."

Now Abram was at her side. He grabbed her arm.

"Stop. You're not going in there. You're going back to the hotel and wait in the lobby like a sane person. When the police are ready they'll come over. Obviously they'll want to ask everyone questions."

Low enough so he hoped she wouldn't hear, he said, "Hell. I knew that ring would bring bad luck."

While she twisted her head to see what was going on behind her, Astrid said, "Huh? What'd you say?"

"Never mind. Just come along."

Three couples, two of them in chairs and one at the front desk, had been watching Abram and Astrid. Their eyes reflected amusement, as did those of Miss Black Eyes, who winked at Abram but quickly turned her attention to her work when Astrid scowled at her,

"You had to cause a scene," she said in Abram's ear.

"Me? We'll sit here and wait," he said calmly.

"Why not? This is where two of the bank robbers sat. Want to play a game of chess?"

"Sure. Why not?"

"You mean you do play?"

Astrid didn't mean to sound so incredulous, but she had never thought to ask if he played the game.

"Sure. Didn't think I was smart enough?"

"No. I didn't mean that. It's just that you never brought it up."

"Nor did you."

"Well, I can't play sitting side to the board."

She got up and turned her chair around. Abram followed suit.

"There," she said. "You want white or black?"

"It's customary to make the draw. Here, I'll do it."

He picked up the white queen and the black one, held his hands behind his back and moved them back and forth between hands.

"There. Pick a hand," he said, holding his fisted hands over the board.

She pointed to the left hand, and he turned it over to reveal the black queen.

"That's the way you picked them up," she said.

"Sure it is. But, you know. A queen rules."

"You never shuffled them."

"Shuffle? You know how to shuffle two chess pieces? If you want white, take them."

"I don't want white. What gave you that idea?"

He pulled in a deep breath and let it out slowly.

"You want to set it up or shall I?"

"Go ahead. I'll keep watch across the street."

"I don't think you'll see a shoot-out today, Dear."

"Abram! You can be so aggravating."

He grinned, and set up her side of the board, then his own. Ready to play, he stopped when she stood up. On the run, she said, "There they are. One car is pulling out already. I have to see them."

With that, she was gone again, and this time Abram let her go. He waited and watched.

He couldn't hear the exchange, but it was plain to see that the officer was annoyed when she began to talk. Astrid had reached him just as he put one foot inside the patrol car. He stood that way for a couple of seconds, but when she grabbed his arm, he stepped out to face his informant up close, eyeball to eyeball. Astrid turned toward the hotel, then the bank. Abram guessed that the officer wanted her to lower her voice when he gestured with a flat hand moving up and down.

More words were exchanged before the officer got into the car and drove away, leaving Astrid with hands on hips, watching the departure. Assuming an indignant swagger, she walked back across the street to the hotel. Abram had the feeling that it didn't go well, and once again he thought, *That damned ring.*

It wasn't that he believed in the curse, he told himself, but it did seem that (aside from the wonderful two days of up close and personal in their room which he recalled with enthusiasm) things had gone badly so far on this honeymoon, starting with the unusually cold weather to the bad accommodations at the previous hotel, and now this encounter with police. He couldn't wait to hear Astrid's tale of woe, which he knew as surely as he knew his own name would include words to the effect...

"Dammit. That cop was rude to me, almost out of control, he got so mad."

Yep. There it was. Just what he anticipated. The policeman was at fault.

"What happened, Dear?"

"He told me to mind my own business. Can you imagine? Police are always telling the public to get involved and report a crime when they see one happening. That's all I was doing. But instead of thanking me and saying he appreciated my sharp eye, what did he do? He insulted me."

She plunked herself on the chair she had vacated so abruptly.

"Why and how did he do that?"

So that everyone in the room wouldn't hear, Abram got up and pulled a chair from the next table to Astrid's side.

"Well, how was I to know? I mean, they looked like robbers to me. Taking guns into the bank and all. The way they played chess, for instance. They had the board set up all wrong, and they were jumping like in checkers and just randomly taking a piece and setting it aside. They weren't playing chess at all. They were watching that bank."

"Okay. And how did the officer insult you?"

"When I told him all this, and that I got a good look at both of them, he said he didn't need me interfering."

"Why? What was going on?"

She looked around to see if anyone was listening.

"It wasn't a robbery at all. The men were undercover cops watching the bank at the time a large cash deposit was coming in. They were watching for the unmarked car so that's when they went over and took up positions inside to be sure there wouldn't be another robbery."

"And that was somehow an insult to you?"

"No. He insulted me when he said he should arrest me for assaulting an officer. Can you believe it? Just because I took hold of his arm. He said I hurt him. Poor man. He needs to get into a physical fitness program. He was flabby."

She looked over at the desk clerk. Abram was quite sure he knew what Astrid was thinking: that woman knew about the operation before she called the police, but did it anyway to embarrass her.

"I don't think she did."

"Did what?"

"Make the call to embarrass you. She had no way of knowing what was going on, did she?"

"Whatever made you think I would even consider that she did that? Really."

Astrid watched out the window for a few seconds then said, "But that *could* be true. Anyway, I'm not going to let this ruin our day. Let's go. I feel like a brisk walk."

He'd had enough briskness at this point. Abram's one thought was how to convince her to return to Fairchance. Nothing had gone right so far and he had little reason to think this honeymoon vacation would get better. Things just didn't go that way around Astrid. The ring didn't enter into his negative thoughts on the matter. He was sure of that.

CHAPTER 5

Blinding sun rays bounced off piles of ice-glazed snow. The few who ventured outside in the near zero frosty air, barred from unplowed sidewalks, slid and slipped along the street. Dee turned from her window overlooking the scene and pouted at Charlie.

"I think I'd rather be in Florida now instead of Fairchance. I can just see Astrid stretched out on a blanket, watching sailboats in the Gulf. I hope she doesn't get a burn. Her skin is so light."

"Weather reporters are saying that a cold front swept through southern states and that many Florida orange crops have been ruined by heavy frosts. If that's so then our honeymooners may never go out of their motel room until it's time to come home."

Dee laughed. "Do they need the cold weather for an excuse?"

"I wouldn't," Charlie said.

"Of course not. You're a man, after all."

"That supposed to be an insult?"

"Oh no. Just an observation. I remember Barry, especially when we were first married."

The silence that followed felt heavy with nostalgia, both Dee and Charlie slipping back in time to the days when they were young and Barry was alive. She still missed him, but her memory had faded to the point that only exceptional scenes with him remained. Now, as the new publisher of *The Bugle*, she had the responsibility of operating the weekly newspaper. More than once she wished Barry were here to help her. Faced with reality, however, Dee accepted the challenge, determined to make it a dynamic publication.

Charlie thought of Barry in terms of strength and fearlessness. He had looked up to Barry but was envious of him, too. When he set his goal to accomplish something, he did it. Dee was lucky to have had him. It was Barry who turned her dream of operating a rehab camp for alcoholics into reality. He designed the entire lakeside complex and then did much of the manual labor to construct it. At the same time, Barry realized his own dream business venture of a pick-your-own strawberry farm. Not just that, but when the camp was finished, he went back to his construction business, building and updating homes for Twin Ports area residents, after he stopped building less profitable, though high-priced, boats. The darkest time of Charlie's life was when Barry died in the hunting camp fire.

"You think your Cat Cotter will make it in today?" he asked, coming back to the present.

He personally felt that this Cat woman was too old to work on *The Bugle*, but had not said so to Dee, since she actually appeared to be considering the possibility. But he himself had found a tighter schedule here than he had as editor of the Twin Ports newspaper, mostly due right now to being so short-handed. Even with a full staff, he had no doubt that this was a busier newspaper than his was. So how could a woman over 70 possibly cope with the pace? No way.

"She isn't *my* Cat Cotter. Not yet, anyway. I would be willing to bet she'll come in today," Dee said. "She strikes me as a determined woman. By-the-way, don't write an editorial for next week. Okay? I want to introduce you to our readers. Since we've already published a story about Natalie's leaving, people have been asking what's going on, who will be editor. We'll run your picture with a page one story. I'll summarize some plans for changes, and hope that we'll have a new reporter on deck. If need be, I'll get Beth Knight to come back again, like I did before you came. She's a lot like Astrid, tall, anyway. But a lot quieter. She's a good reporter. I wouldn't mind having her full time, but she says she won't do that. Anyway, if I don't write about the changes, I do have something else all ready to go."

"Blamed if I know what I'd write, anyway, so you're a life-saver."

"If you find yourself in that predicament any time—that you don't have an editorial subject—just let me know. I can usually come up with something. There are a few topics on the back burner that haven't been discussed yet."

"Ayuh, I'll do that. I'll need that boost now and again until I get acquainted with goings on here. You actually have plans for changes already?'

"Not really, but as I write, I'm sure some ideas will sprout."

When the door opened ten minutes later, Dee looked over expecting to see the wannabe reporter. Instead, Marvin Cornell walked in. He had gained weight finally, after the long grieving period for his wife, and now looked like his old vibrant self. He took off his fur-lined winter cap and dropped it on Astrid's desk. Dee noticed that his hair was stylishly longer than the last time she talked with him, about two months ago. The long vacation had given him badly needed rest. Obviously the Mediterranean cruise was what he needed. Dee almost wished she had taken him up on his offer for her to go with him, but who would have run the newspaper if she had gone?

"Welcome home, Marvin," she said. "You're looking great. I guess the cruise suited."

"Indeed it did." He went to Charlie. "And I guess you're the new editor."

Standing, he said, "Yes, sir. Charlie Hart."

"Welcome to Fairchance, Charlie. I'm the former publisher Marvin Cornell, now just the proprietor of the commercial print shop. Dee tells me that you're the right person for the job, and I have to believe that's true. She never lies."

He looked at Dee and winked. She saw the old sparkle in his eyes, maybe due to the sale of the newspaper, but more likely the result of a restful vacation from everything. It couldn't be anything to do with her, surely.

"You're right there," Charlie said. "I've known her more than 20 years. I don't ever recall that she told a falsehood."

"You're both mistaken, but we'll leave it at that," she said. "So you had a good cruise, Marvin."

"My dear, you have to do it sometime. Not only are the ports of call breathtaking, but the ship itself is unbelievable. And the food is out of this world. I must have put on ten pounds."

He sat in the visitor's chair next to Charlie's desk and pushed it away enough to look at both comfortably.

"That did you no harm," Dee said. "May I take your coat?"

"No, no. I won't stay but a minute. I know Monday is a busy news day for you. Have you heard from the honeymooners yet?"

"Not yet. Charlie and I were just talking about them and wondering how the weather is affecting their visit to Florida. The word is that it's cold there."

"I heard that, too. Just came over the radio. In northern parts of Florida it went down to the teens. Hard to believe Florida's in deep freeze. Lucky it doesn't happen often. It's too bad for Astrid and her new husband. But to get on with it, I do have a purpose in coming in, Dee. There's a little problem in our transfer papers we signed before I left. So will you come over to the shop so we can fix it?"

"Anything serious?"

"No. Just a couple of places where we didn't sign our initials. An oversight by the attorney's secretary."

"Do you need me now?"

"No, no. Johnson will be dropping by at 4:30 today, if that's convenient for you."

"Oh sure. I'll be there. In your office, then?"

"In my office. It's good to be back. I didn't think much about the shop while I was traveling, but as soon as I got back, I had to come over and see that everything was going smoothly."

"With Rene running things, I'm sure it was."

"Right. He's my right-hand man. Been with me many years."

He got up, put the chair back in place, and retrieved his hat.

"So I'll see you at about 4:30. Carry on."

After wishing Charlie well, Marvin left. Dee studied the story she'd just written, hoping Charlie wouldn't quiz her about her relationship with Marvin. Of course, she told herself, there was no relationship. But still when he looked at her so intently just now, anyone might have read something into it. And that was just ridiculous. She didn't even get a postcard from him while he was gone.

"Hello," the voice sang before the door was fully open. "I got here."

Unwinding a long scarf from her face and taking off her mittens, Cat Cotter sailed across the editorial room to Dee's desk and pulled a folder from her briefcase. Dee could feel a halo of frigid air when she leaned over to put the folder on her desk.

"I brought you a story I wrote. I know you didn't assign it, but it just seemed to fall in my lap and I knew you wouldn't mind. After all, you just want to see if I can write, I suspect."

"Well, this is a surprise. All typed out, too. Just take a chair and warm up. Better still, Charlie why don't you take Cat to the lounge and give her a hot drink. Coffee is all made or you can make hot chocolate, if you prefer. There are some sweets, too."

"I would enjoy a cup of coffee," Cat said.

Dee began reading the first of three pages the woman had written. By the third page, she said, "Oh my God," and yelled, "Charlie!"

He came to the door. "You want me?"

"Close the door and come over here. Bring that chair so you can sit by me."

He did as she said, leaned his elbows on the desk, and said, "What's up, boss?"

She was close to saying, "Stop that," but let it go. It was the second time he'd called her boss, and he had to know how much she hated it.

"This story that Cat wrote. Take a look."

When he finished, he pushed the pages back to her and whistled. Charlie had not changed a great deal over the years, a bit outlandish at times, always ready for an adventure, devious and never stumped for a way to get a story. How well Dee remembered *that*. He still had the extreme downeast drawl.

"You think this is true?" he said.

"I don't know. I've lived in Maine most of my life, and never once have I seen mention of this sort of thing in any newspaper. Never even heard casual gossip about it, either. Seems bizarre to me."

"It's bizarre, all right. Maybe our Cat is writing fiction instead of news, you think? What do you want to do about it, boss?"

"Give it up, Charlie," Dee said, giving him a nudge. "We're working together, at least until Astrid gets back. Don't call me boss anyway. I don't like it. I don't know exactly what to do, but they're located in the western part of the county. Since you were slated to be editor for that area, I think you should investigate."

"I hope you're not demoting me now just because I called you boss."

"Don't be silly, Charlie. Of course not." Then she looked up and saw his grin. "This investigation is more of a man's job, I think. If what she writes is true, a woman could be intimidated more easily than a man. What do you think?"

"Could be."

"Will you bring her back in? I'll have to talk with her about it."

Charlie went to the lounge door and opened it.

"Come in, Cat. We need to discuss your story."

She left her cup on the round lunch table and walked past Charlie. Her bounce still surprised him, given her age. Despite his concern over what she had written, he smiled.

Dee wanted to yell, *What do you think you're doing, woman?*

Instead she took a breath and in a calm voice said, "This is a startling story, Cat. We need to do some editing, and to double check everything you've said here. How long have you known about it? If it exists, that is."

Cat stiffened where she sat in the chair that Charlie had vacated.

"Oh, I can assure you I wrote nothing but the truth. This really does exist, and we're all in serious danger."

"Maybe that's so, but we have to be careful about editorializing in our news stories. You must know that, given your background as a journalist. Let's start at the beginning. You write, 'The Ku Klux Klan is alive and well right here in Lanier County.' That's inflammatory language, and may be an exaggeration, I'm afraid."

"Well, it certainly is *not* an exaggeration. Maybe you don't think a militia group is KKK, but I do. It's the same thing. They'll murder anyone who doesn't agree with them. I tell you, we are all in danger of being shot in the street, or in our beds. We need to have every last one of those outlaws arrested and hanged…or at least given life in prison."

Dee sat back, shocked at Cat's passion, the extreme action she would have the law take, and the very suggestion that the city would be invaded by men with guns. Hoping to get at the veracity of the remarks, Dee held up her hand for the woman to stop.

"First of all, Maine doesn't have capital punishment any more. But what I need to know is where did you get this information?"

"I believe I should protect my sources."

That haughty air and knife-sharp voice sent Dee over the edge of calm decorum. She had encountered too many with attitude at the rehab camp not to know when someone was trying to control the situation. Cat obviously thought she could waltz in and demand newspaper space for her call to arms story.

"Protect your sources? That's not a statement you make to the publisher who you want to print your story and possibly hire you. I can't and won't publish a story without knowing where it came from. Nor will I hire anyone without knowing more than I know now. So, since you didn't give attribution in the story, you can either tell me who gave you this information or you can take your story with you as you leave."

Cat's shoulders slumped and she looked down. Her head moved back and forth as she tried to make up her mind. Dee could see the inner conflict. Should she bend and do as Dee demanded, or should she just do the alternate ultimatum--walk out? Dee was sure of one thing. The publisher was the boss and she would *be* the boss, even if she didn't want Charlie to call her that.

"I see." The sigh was of surrender. "Well, if you must know, I live next door to Mr. Kinsley, the funeral director. I'm sure you know that he's also the county coroner. A couple of weeks ago, he was called by the Greenboro undertaker, who had fallen from his roof and broken his leg and is incapacitated. He wanted Mr. Kinsley to pick up a body from a nearby place called The Kingdom, like I wrote. Mr. Kinsley said the man had died outside the camp and he didn't see anything beyond a tool shed in the woods where they had taken him. But what he saw there shocked him. The place was lined with guns."

She reached over and snatched her story from Dee's desk.

"This was a training camp. He'd seen one before in Mississippi, where guns were stored like that, and the men gathered in the woods. That one was a KKK camp where white supremacists indoctrinated recruits for their acts of terror. When he asked the man who seemed to be in charge what they needed so many guns for, he replied that they had a militia camp not far away. You see, they didn't want him snooping around."

She stood up, paced to Astrid's desk and back, twice. Dee let her go. She could see that Cat needed to vent her excitement, and waited until she collected her thoughts. But she wasn't prepared for what followed.

"You want to live?"

Cat opened her bag and took out a small pistol, pointed it at Dee, who held up her hand in a gesture of self-protection. Charlie stood up, ready to lunge.

"Then don't let this happen to you. Don't let these outlaws, these madmen with a distorted idea of freedom and the American way come in here and hold a gun on you like this, and tell you they are taking over."

She put the gun away, while Dee and Charlie looked at each other, their wide eyes silently questioning the sanity of this woman.

"I wrote it as Mr. Kinsley told me," she waved her story as if she were brushing away flies, "and I believe him. I believe it is a militia, being trained right here in this county to take over towns and cities and eliminate all those who are not of their color and ethnicity. I would not be surprised if there were more throughout this state that are being trained and gathering firearms, for a unified assault. This is a nation-wide movement. Haven't you read about these Patriot gangs?"

Dee had to stop her. No knowing what she'd do if she didn't calm down.

"All right, all right. I understand. There are still several things that have to be done before we can break a story like this. First of all, you and anyone else who knows about it must stay mum. You must not spread fear, or else pandemonium could break out with mob action worse than these supposed terrorists would bring. A story like this has to be well documented, absolutely corroborated by authorities before we can publish it."

She motioned for Cat to sit down again next to her.

"I'm not rejecting the story. I'm simply telling you what we must do. When the time comes for the news to break, I will be sure that you are given the credit you deserve. So please, whatever you do, stay quiet. Just wait until we can do what we must do from this end. Understand? Will you do that?"

Cat's whole demeanor softened. She nodded.

"Does this mean I have the job?"

"No. Not yet, anyway. I appreciate your zeal, but in a case like this, you should always consult the editor before going after the story. For now, you agree to keep a lid on it?"

"I do. You don't have to worry. Mr. Kinsley has already said he wouldn't say anything about this to anyone. He wanted me to have the chance to write the story. I'll tell him that we are working on the details."

Dee smiled and again exchanged glances with Charlie.

"Yes. That's best."

As she was leaving, Cat turned her head and said, "This isn't a real gun, you know. It's a cigarette lighter. Looks like the real thing, though, doesn't it?"

Dee was breathing hard when Cat left. She couldn't remember being so shaken by anyone, except for the time she had to defend her life using an empty sardine can for a weapon. So many years ago.

Charlie was the first to break their silence.

"Now what will we do? You believe that group is a terrorist outfit? I wonder if the sheriff is investigating."

Dee fought to control her voice.

"That's what we need to find out. I'll call the sheriff, since I know him. But I want you to think about the possibility of going to the camp, maybe stay a day or two. Think you could do it?"

"Sure. I've been with worse."

"I wish Astrid was coming home sooner than another two weeks. We could really use her help."

"Why don't you call her and ask how she's doing. If she sounds bored with the vacation now that she's been there a while, tell her how much you miss her and how much you wish she were here to help."

"And break off her honeymoon? That would be cruel."

"Maybe. Maybe not. You could try, anyway. Jen and I didn't have a honeymoon, and we're still happily married."

"We'll see. About Astrid, that is."

A cruise was everyone's dream. She couldn't deny the couple that pleasure, nor would she even hint at it.

To change the subject, she said, "We've been so busy, I haven't had a chance to ask if you found a place to live on the weekend."

Charlie nodded toward the window.

"I did find one place I liked. Jenny will come over tomorrow, if the roads are all clear, and we'll go looking together." His voice dropped to almost a whisper. "I miss her."

"Tomorrow morning I'll go see the sheriff," Dee said before leaving. "Even if there is a militia group near here, I don't want to publish a story until you've had time to go out there and find out more. This is the type of story that must be handled with discretion so we don't find ourselves being accused of printing lies on the one hand, or undermining authorities on the other. And we don't need a law suit right away, either. This peaceful community could be turned into a gang of vigilantes without much provocation, I fear. Have you ever seen a Mainer without an opinion or a solution to the most serious problems? And I would hazard a guess that every house in Fairchance has a gun in a closet or a nightstand. We need to treat this with kid gloves."

"I agree," Charlie said. "So do you think you can hire Cat Cotter yet? We're going to need help if we're to do an in-depth story like this."

"I know. No. I've got to try to find someone else. I don't know if I want her at all, but for sure not before we get the poop on this armed group in the boonies. She very well could be out there doing who knows what…maybe convincing herself she should become a sniper and pick off one or two men from a blind somewhere near their camp. I don't know. But I'll tell you one thing. The students she taught were nowhere near as afraid of her as I am."

After she left for the day, Charlie mulled over that conversation while he debated with himself on a course of action. They had a very real problem here, and it would be impossible for him to perform the dual roles of reporter and editor while tactfully approaching the leaders of the group with its questionable intentions, hidden away from society, and playing at whatever they were playing with dangerous weapons. The obvious solution would be to call Astrid, explain all this to her, and plead with her to take her honeymoon at a more appropriate time.

But Dee hadn't wanted to do that. He understood. Women were born romantics, reading magic into the beginning of a marriage, magic that apparently could work successfully only after a proper honeymoon. Amazing that he and Jenny had lived all these years so happily without going to some exotic place and receiving the anointing waters.

Nevertheless, he knew he had to try to get Astrid back. Anointed or not, she'd have to weave magic into her marriage somehow without another week of the honeymoon. But wait. The cruise. Hell, he couldn't do that. He couldn't make them miss a cruise. His own dream was to one day take Jenny on a cruise. No, he just wouldn't do that. Would he?

CHAPTER 6

By the morning when they were to take the cruise, Astrid had bought herself two sweaters and a fleece jacket as the weather continued to spread a gloomy pall over what should be the happiest days of her life. She refused to feel cheated by it, however, and moved about the hotel room quickly to lay out her clothes for the day, did some calisthenics, brushed and braided her hair. After a hot shower, she found Abram still curled up under the sheet and blanket, reluctant to leave the meager warmth of the bed.

"Time to get up, Abram," she said. "We need to be ready for the bus to Fort Lauderdale to catch our ship. I'll finish the packing while you're showering. Just think. Tonight we'll be on the sea."

"This cruise. Tell me again why we're doing it? I get seasick, you know."

"Because we're in Florida, and we want to do as much as we can now. We won't be coming this way again for a long while, I expect."

"Too soon for me," he said, making sure she didn't hear.

"What's that?"

"Nothing. That's a nice sweater. Blue is your color."

She smiled at him. He said that too quickly. Covering up for some derogatory remark, no doubt, and she could guess. All he did yesterday was grumble about his disappointment in Florida, weather too cold to go to the beach, and rude people. She'd like to dispute his complaints, but in truth he was right, especially about the rude people around them. Did they get into some sort of sub culture here? Or was it the weather that made everyone testy?

A haunting question, above all else, was should they even be here? That was the creepiest part of it all. Her sense told her their honeymoon rhythm had gone berserk, like a waltz and a conga played at the same time, completely out of sync. That shouldn't be.

They loved each other, but everything around them tended to unsettle their tranquility. At every site they visited, even here at the hotel, an innocent move or a well-meaning comment was twisted. At a check-out for a few snacks, she put the separator behind her purchases and the next person's items, and the man behind her said, "You shuttin' me out, whitey?" As insulting as the remark was, Astrid said nothing, though she felt like bopping him one in the nose. Another time, Abram took a woman's arm to help her step onto a store escalator. She yanked her arm away and shouted, "Watch it, mister," as if he were accosting her.

"Crazy." Standing at the window and looking at the cold Gulf water, Astrid didn't realize she had said it aloud.

"What?"

"Huh?"

"You said crazy. What's crazy?"

"Oh, nothing in particular. Just thinking out loud."

They had been here a week. How could so much go wrong in that time? Wouldn't it have been better if they had taken a week off and gone skiing at Sugarloaf? They would have been dressed for the weather, and undoubtedly have enjoyed themselves more. She wished they had done that.

Casablanca was a favorite old movie of Astrid's and she barely noticed the passing swamps and emptiness through which Alligator Alley connects the west coast from Naples to the east coast at Fort Lauderdale, or anything else going on as she watched the movie playing on the bus. Until she smelled it.

"My God, Abram, what *is* that awful odor? Smells like…"

"Yeah. Poor old guy behind us. I don't know why a woman would drag her husband along for a cruise when he's old and sick."

"They're going on a cruise?"

"I heard a woman across the aisle say so. She's really upset. She's talking with the driver now. Can you see?"

"Ya, I see. What does she expect the driver to do?"

"I think she wants him to put the couple off."

"Well, where are we? They can't get off here. It's in the middle of nowhere."

"Precisely. Let's see what happens."

Several miles later, the driver stopped the bus and walked down to the older couple, helped the woman get her husband up, down the aisle with his walker, and off the bus. They were at a small town.

"Poor thing," Astrid said. "So hard to grow old. I wonder what she'll do now."

"She'll find a way. Women always do."

From out of nowhere, two men with mops and pails came down the aisle and cleaned up the mess the old man had made. Finally, the bus started up again. They could hear passengers complaining that they'd be late arriving. The air became tolerable, but Astrid thought about the incident with misgivings. She remembered her dear grandfather when he got to that stage of losing control. Body functions were one thing, but for him being weak and not able to get up or direct life around him was the bigger humiliation. He said to her once that it was no way to live. Gunnar thought their grandfather might commit suicide rather than go on like a total baby, but Astrid knew better. From then on she stayed with him until he breathed his last.

"We're at the port."

Abram's voice jarred Astrid from her reverie, and she realized she had missed the movie's exit scene. Looking around she saw the gigantic ships, cars coming and going, and people running to and from who-knew-where.

"It's a big place," she said.

The adventure had cooled for her, and she knew she never should have scheduled the cruise. Abram had no love for the water, the weather forecaster had announced that the cold weather would go into next week, and she suddenly felt tired, exhausted from all the sightseeing they had done during the past week up and down the west coast of Florida. She was tired of this whole schedule.

They were directed to the terminal where they waited in line to go inside. Nothing was moving toward boarding yet, they were told. Astrid and Abram found a bench to sit on and pulled their luggage as tightly as possible to their feet.

"Don't you hate waiting?" The sixtyish woman sitting next to Astrid asked.

"Ya. I do. Have you been waiting long?"

"I've been here since morning. I came to meet a friend and her husband who were returning from another cruise, and I took them home, just a few miles down 95. She said they had a terrible cruise. They both got sick, the water was that rough. The ship's pool was slopping around and spilling out over the deck, so it was dangerous walking on the lido deck. And they couldn't get off at more than one port of call. When they did, they about froze. I've never seen a winter like this myself. Lived here for nine years, and it has always been perfect weather when we cruised. Have you taken many cruises?"

"No. This is our first."

"Be sure to take a pill for seasickness before we start out tonight. The roughest part of the cruise is around the Keys in the Florida straits."

Astrid looked at Abram to see if he had heard. He had.

"What do you think?" she asked. He understood her meaning.

"If you're thinking what I am, we should skip it and head back to the hotel."

"Ya. There'll be another time, some year. We don't have to suffer this one out just to say we did it. Let's find the place where we can catch a bus going back to the west coast."

By early evening, they were back at the hotel, heading for the elevator when the desk clerk called out to Astrid.

"A message was left for you, Mrs. Lincoln."

"A message? Who in the world…?"

She went to the desk and took the note with nothing more than a telephone number on it.

"It's a 207 area code, so it's someone from home," she said, as they entered the elevator and Abram pressed the button for the eighth floor.

"I hope no one is sick. If Dee is sick, I'll have to go back, Abram. She's alone except for the new editor."

"Sure. No problem. I think we're both ready to go home anyway."

"Ya, I think so, too. This number looks familiar. I think it's the Edge of Town Motel. Don't you?"

He looked at it.

"Yes, it is. Who do you know there now?"

"No one. I don't think I do." A moment later, "Oh, I do. It may be Charlie. He's probably staying there. Oh dear, now I'm really worried that Dee's sick, or something awful has happened."

She fidgeted until the elevator stopped and she could get off. In the room, she quickly dialed the number.

"Edge of Town Motel. Patti speaking. May I help you?"

"Patti, it's Astrid."

"How are you Astrid? Still on your honeymoon?"

"Ya, and I'm fine. Someone called me from there."

"That's Charlie Hart. I'll ring his room for you."

When he answered, Astrid hastily said, "What's wrong, Charlie? This is Astrid, returning your call."

"Hi Astrid. How's your honeymoon going?"

"Fine, thanks. But you didn't call to ask that."

"No. Well," he hesitated. "You see, we have a situation."

"Is Dee sick? The office burn down? What?"

"No, no. Everyone's okay. The office building is still standing. But we're short-handed, as you know, and Dee hasn't been able to hire anyone yet. Now, it seems there's something going on over west of Greenboro, and she wants me to go there and spend a bit of time to find out if it's dangerous, or just what it's all about."

"I don't understand. What *is* going on?"

"It's a long story, but I'll give it to you briefly. Seems there's some kind of militia group that's sprung up. They've built a community in the woods and according to what we heard, it's a regular army training type operation. We can fill you in later. Now understand, Dee didn't want to ask you to come back. She knew you've scheduled a cruise. In fact, I thought you might be gone today."

"No. We decided not to go. It's just too cold and windy."

"Well, I don't want to break up your honeymoon."

"Don't worry about that."

"If you come back, it would probably be better not to mention this call to Dee."

"It never happened."

After hanging up, Astrid sat thinking for only a second before saying, "Sorry Dear, I guess we need to pack and go home. I'll call the airline ticket office now."

Abram wasted no time plopping his case on the bed and trying not to smile too broadly while he packed. The reason for the sudden change of plans didn't concern him in the least. He was getting out of this dreadful "paradise" and going home.

CHAPTER 7

Wednesday morning was a welcome five degrees warmer than it had been for over a week, with bright sunshine still too thin and too weak to melt hoar frost, but welcome after three days of cloudy sky. Dee left her car and crunched over broken ice to the back door of the old Cape, hurried down the hallway, and was surprised to find Charlie already tapping away at his computer, sipping hot coffee between spurts of inspiration. His hair, as always, looked frozen in wisps of gray, as if he'd showered and gone outside without drying it. Amazing how much older he looked, with deep lines around his mouth and between heavy eyebrows, probably because he loved to work outdoors and to fish and hunt. Most of their friends looked younger. She herself had some gray in her black hair but only laugh lines around her eyes, while Jenny probably never would look or be old, she was so enthusiastic about life in general. She was ever an exception. As a teenager, Dee remembered her friend's doll-like beauty complete with blond hair. How happy everyone was the day Charlie announced that Jenny would become his wife.

"You're early today." she said. "Is that coffee I smell? This *is* a special day."

"Savor it now. It may never happen again. Just wanted to get a head start on things before I go out to The Kingdom, if I am going, that is. Did you talk with Sheriff Knight yet?"

For some reason he didn't understand, she had been putting off that discussion. He had begun to think the whole story might be a hoax. Then yesterday when he asked about it, she said she would see the sheriff after work.

"I did. Let me get coffee and then I'll tell you. But I want to know when you and Jenny are moving to Fairchance. This coming weekend?"

"I don't know for sure. She's anxious to, and so am I. It depends on how much she can get packed, and whether she can get everything ready on that end in Twin Ports. Moving is not a simple matter."

"No. I know. Well good luck and if there's anything I can do to help, let me know."

She went to the lounge, leaving the door open.

"Want a sweet roll, Charlie?" she called.

"Ayuh. That would be good."

She poured her coffee and checked to see if the filter was still in the top of the maker. It was. Did men ever take care of such details, she wondered. She threw it in the wastebasket, got two paper plates from the overhead cupboard, and put a roll on each, then returned and set one plate in front of Charlie.

"Want me to get you more coffee?" she said.

"No thanks. I'm fine."

She was barely settled before he asked, "So what did Sheriff Knight say? Have they been investigating? Did he say how the group started up and what they plan to do?"

The coffee and roll were her breakfast, so she talked while chewing.

"He's aware of their activity, and isn't too happy about it. But since they aren't breaking any laws that he knows about, there's no reason to investigate more than he has. They've been there for some time, though he wasn't sure just how long. They didn't come to his attention until that man died—the one Cat Cotter spoke of. He did talk with the man who calls himself general out there. Larry said he's affable enough and assured him they were harmless. He supposed it was nothing more than a campsite for tents and weekend war games."

"Charming. I look forward to the experience of meeting them. Did you mean that he already has investigated them?"

"He has checked with the FBI. They have nothing on the general or the group."

"So I'm still going to tent city?"

"Yes, but I think we should wait just a few days."

"Sure. In the meantime, I'll get some aerosol spray. Could be gamey out there."

Charlie's sarcastic tone didn't escape Dee's notice. She said no more, but wondered if he secretly regretted having come to Fairchance to work for her. He had been the editor in Twin Ports, and while it was a lateral move, there must be times when he regretted that he hadn't been able to stop the takeover of his own newspaper. Of course, his salary wasn't as high here as previously, another set-back. Then again, he could be concerned about what her role would be in the upcoming weeks. Would she be here in the editorial room, giving orders to everyone, or would she go to her upstairs office and leave control in his hands? She wished she knew the answer to that one herself. One thing she knew was that she would always want to write even if no more than an occasional editorial. Maybe she'd begin her own weekly column.

Her phone buzzed and Billie in the business office said, "Dee, it's Cat Cotter."

"Oh," Dee sighed before pressing the line. "Cat, what can I do for you today?"

"Well, I've been waiting to hear from you. I didn't see anything in the newspaper this week. Have you done anything about those terrorists out in Greenboro?"

"Cat, we're not calling them terrorists until and if there's reason to. And, yes. I've done something. I've discussed the matter with Sheriff Knight. We plan to pursue the investigation. If I have reason to call you in, I will."

She was trying to be firm, but Cat was a hard woman to be firm with, even over the telephone. When Cat spoke, it felt like she was ready to crack a whip: Snap! *Listen to me. I'm in charge here.*

But she wasn't in charge, and Dee must be on her guard.

"You're taking enough time, it seems to me," Cat said. "I should be there to help you. I can come in today or tomorrow."

"No!" Dee realized she had shouted the word, more out of fear of seeing Cat come through the door in 15 minutes than anything else. "We're doing just fine, and like I said, if I need you, I'll call you."

"And you don't want me to do anything? Just sit at home and wait by the phone when I could contribute to the investigation?"

How could she get it across to this woman that that's exactly what she wanted her to do?

"It's the best way for now. You've alerted us to the possible problem, and we and the sheriff's department are all working on it. So just be patient. I don't need you right now."

She expected a sharp response to that, but instead, she waited through silence until finally Cat said, "All right. I'll wait."

Without a goodbye, she hung up.

Shaking her head, Dee said, "That's a difficult woman to figure out, Charlie. Just when I thought she'd give me a bitter argument, she said okay, she'd wait."

"If we don't do something soon, she'll be camping out on our doorstep. Not to change the subject, but I've been thinking about that construction work they plan to start out by the motel where I'm staying. Do you know what it's all about?"

"I wasn't aware of any construction."

"Sign out front of a high fence says 'Coming Soon, Strippers.' But nothing's coming off right now"

"Now Charlie."

But she had to laugh just the same.

"Strippers," she said. "Never heard of it. We'll have to check it out with the Zoning Board. But I'm not sure if there is any special zoning out there. If only…"

"If only what?"

"Oh nothing."

What she almost said was 'If only Astrid were here, she'd go at it and have answers in no time.'

"It's lunch time, Charlie. Go ahead. I'll wait until one o'clock. I want to check out that new sub shop downtown."

"Good idea. I think I'll do the same. I'll let you know how it is."

"Well, why don't you bring me a sub? Here, take this."

She handed him a five dollar bill.

"What do you want?"

"Turkey with all the stuff except onions and peppers. Okay?"

"Okay. Be back about five."

"Better not be."

She heard voices in the hallway as he was leaving, turned to her computer and began typing. When the door opened and Astrid walked in, she couldn't find her voice at first, but stared at her in disbelief.

"I hope that look of horror on your face is a good sign," Astrid said.

"Oh, my goodness. Astrid. What are you doing here? You're supposed to be on cruise."

"We got cold feet, literally. Seemed like north was the better direction to go. If we had to be cold, at least we'd be more comfortable at home."

"But I thought the farther south you go, the warmer it is."

"So did I, but that wasn't the case this year. It was cold and windy everywhere and we likely wouldn't be able to go to a beach for swimming, We'd already had enough of that in Florida so why go sailing down the Atlantic when we couldn't even get onto the ship's decks without being blown away. To top it off, Abram gets seasick. It was a sure thing he'd find that condition less than pleasant. So here we are, where it's cold and invigorating and nice."

Dee wanted to hug Astrid for making that choice. Instead, she said, "Believe me, you are more welcome than you can imagine. I still haven't hired a new reporter. Charlie and I have been doing it all, and to top it off we have a rather odd woman who wants to join the staff. Wait until you hear."

CHAPTER 8

Astrid hadn't felt so welcome in a very long time, and it buoyed her morale almost as much as the first night she and Abram spent in the same bed in their rented Fairchance home. Obviously Dee needed her, too.

At first, Dee rambled a bit telling about this Cat Cotter and her worries about The Kingdom militia, but soon she calmed down, apparently realizing that it really was Astrid, and that she'd be here a good long while, ready to work.

Interrupting her own discourse, Dee said, "Now, maybe we can settle down to more than just the nitty gritty. I've made a list of stories that need to be developed. Choose what appeals to you. If you prefer I can make the assignments, but you usually know as well as I do what's priority and what's not."

Astrid read the list aloud.

"A new sub shop--oh, good--a used book exchange shop, Catholic Church renovation. What's this? Strippers? You kidding?"

"I have no idea what that is. Charlie said there's a sign out by The Edge of Town Motel that says 'Coming Soon, Strippers.'"

Astrid laughed. "A play on words, no doubt. The town fathers would squelch that project in a flash if it meant a strip club."

Going back to the list, she said, "Rather short list, isn't it?"

"Not much going on this time of year. Of course, the schools and college need to be checked often. We can sort out who'll do what when Charlie gets back."

"What will Charlie do at that place--what did you call it? The Kingdom?"

"The Kingdom, yes. Maybe he won't do anything more than interview a few of those who live there. He may not be welcome, for that matter. It wouldn't surprise me. We want to find out what they're doing or plan to do. Sheriff Knight knows about it, but hasn't seen it. And this Cat Cotter...well, she insists they're on the order of the Ku Klux Klan and that we all stand to be murdered in our beds if we don't close them down, kick them out."

"Cat Cotter. I remember that name from somewhere. But where?"

Astrid concentrated on the name.

"No. I can't think of it now, but it will come to me sometime. I'm sure I've run into that name before."

"She worked for the *Christian Science Monitor* for some time. I'd say she writes well from what I read of her clips. I don't know how well she'd fit into our routine. As for her personality, I can't say that I found her particularly likable. She comes on like gangbusters. Believe it or not, she pulled a fake gun, a cigarette lighter...you know what I mean. Charlie and I thought it was real. She's lucky Charlie didn't tackle her."

"Why did she do that?"

"Wanted to emphasize a point. She thinks we're all in danger from these terrorists, as she calls them. She was demonstrating how it would be if they decided to take over everything. She believes that will happen, that there are more than this one camp of them, and their ultimate goal is to overturn the government."

Astrid slapped her hand on the desk, Charlie's desk, where she was sitting.

"Now I know where I've heard that name. Oh, Dee, keep her out of here. She's trouble. When I was working for a small newspaper outside Syracuse, a column came to my desk through the mail. It looked legitimate enough, supposedly syndicated by the *Christian Science Monitor*. After I read it, I took it to the editor and let him read it. He told me to throw it in the wastebasket, and I did. I still remember how it was titled: *America, You Will Soon Be Under Attack*. And it went on with a frightening description of a new uprising called United Patriots. The column said that this group planned domestic bombings and raids until the United States would finally be taken over by non-tax-paying Patriots."

Astrid paused to breathe. She gazed down Main Street for a few seconds, enjoying the deep freeze of winter. She simply was a northerner and a farm girl, there was no denying it.

She said, "A peaceful city like Fairchance would have civil war within its own boundaries. Can you imagine? And the author of that outrageous column was Cat Cotter."

"The *Monitor* syndicated the column?"

"No, of course not. She was just using the name for her own ends. When the *Monitor* started receiving letters asking what was going on, they fired her. I don't know what that camp in the woods is all about, but I do know that she's a rabble rouser. As I understand it, she's been fired from more than one job. A friend of mine, who works for another paper in New York, told me that."

"I had already decided not to hire her. I guess my instincts were right. She's just too demanding to begin with. Practically moved in before I had a chance to talk with her. Now I'm *really* glad you came back. But, tell me, why didn't you wait for it to warm up in Florida? It would, you know."

Astrid was about to describe the conditions when Charlie came in, carrying a bag of subs and chips. He looked at her and winked, being careful not to let Dee see it.

"Welcome back to the North Pole, Astrid," he said. "You didn't get much of a tan."

"Oh, please," she said. "You can't imagine how disappointed we were in Florida, and all that went with it. Too cold to even go out in the sun or to swim or do much of anything else. We were told what a disaster the cruise would be by a woman who got it first-hand from a friend on her return from the previous cruise. So we just canceled it all and went back to the hotel, and decided it was more fun here than there. So here we are."

She made no mention of the telephone call from Charlie. She'd tell him later how much she appreciated his call, however. Though she and Abram wanted to return, cutting two weeks off their honeymoon, neither said as much. Would they have returned early? Maybe. But when Charlie called, she had the perfect reason and knew it was the right thing to do.

"What about Abram?" Dee asked. "Is he back at work, too?"

"He will be. He talked with the sheriff this morning and was told to report for work on the two to ten shift Friday. I don't know how long he'll be doing that, but it's a good shift for him. Gives him the morning to do what he wants, after getting a good night's sleep. Anyway, he works only four days a week, you know. Just a part-time job for him for now."

"At least he's on the mend, and probably lighter work is best for him now."

"Ya. In the spring, he'll start building our new home. He has some wonderful ideas for it."

"Hey, you two, let's dig into these subs," Charlie said on his way to the lounge. "I'll make a fresh pot of coffee."

Astrid couldn't help but think how much had happened since she came to Fairchance and took this job, just five months ago.

And now, here she was a married woman, really feeling at home, with a new boss and a new editor, all so comfortable, and all so right. It gave her a warm and contented feeling. But it would most likely not last long, if the past was any indication of the future.

****

Lunch over, and telephone calls under way for interviews, the editorial room went from tranquil to tumultuous the second Cat Cotter burst through the door across from Astrid. Bundled in wools, boots, and mittens, the woman wasted no time getting to the point.

"I told you! I told you this would happen!"

She scurried across to Dee and stood, legs apart and flat-footed, waving a mitten inches from her face.

"Sure as God made little green apples, I told you these people should be stopped. But no. No one listened to me. Now look at what you've let happen."

Dee stood up and pushed back her chair, in a challenging mode.

"What did I let happen, Cat? What are you talking about?'

"You dragged your feet, instead of forewarning the public about that militia bunch. Now, they've attacked."

"Attacked? Who attacked? Where? When?"

"Huh! Now you act like a reporter. You should have been asking those questions a week ago. I could have done that. I could have routed them out of their hiding places in the woods, and they could have been locked away."

Cat flipped off her scarf, like a stage performer, and lifted her chin in defiance.

"But no. Now they've come to town and robbed the City Bank. That's what they've done."

Astrid shuddered when she heard the word bank.

"When did this happen?" Dee asked.

"Just five minutes ago. I was walking along Main Street, going for milk and bread, when I saw them, wearing Halloween masks, two of them, small men…"

Dee didn't wait, but talked over Cat's chatter. However, Astrid heard the words, "They were running along the street in front of the bank."

Dee was saying, "Charlie, take your camera to the bank and see what you can find out. Astrid, call the police station and ask some questions. In the meantime, you go home, Cat. And remember, until we know what has happened and who the thieves are, I ask you not to say or do anything about it. Let the police do their work before passing judgment. Please."

"Well. I thought I might get a thank-you, at least. But you are all so busy that you didn't even have your scanner on, I see."

She was right there, but Astrid spoke up for Dee.

"No, Cat. We didn't, and it's my fault. I returned from my honeymoon early, and we had much to talk about. So nice to meet you. Let me see you to the door."

Taking the woman's arm, Astrid looked down at her and said, "You've done your deed for the day."

She deliberately omitted the word good when she said deed, her own opinion of the woman being too low to even imply there was anything good about her actions.

Looking up at Astrid, Cat said, "And who are you?"

"I'm a reporter. Astrid Lincoln. Do you need a ride home?"

"No. I don't need a ride. Been walking since I was eight months old. If I need help, I'll say so. What kind of name is Astrid?"

"Swedish."

"I didn't know we had Swedes in Maine. Where are you from?"

"East of Rockland. A native Mainer."

"Well. Very indefinite, I must say."

"Definite enough."

"You don't look like a reporter. More like a basketball coach."

Astrid smiled.

Apparently stunned by the brush off and the voice and height of Astrid, Cat said no more. But that was okay, Astrid thought. This woman may or may not have seen a bank robbery, but she wanted to start work on the story. As for herself, she knew all too well that bank robberies sometimes were not what they seemed, but rather merely a figment of an over-active imagination. She admired Dee for her level head and her tolerance of an obviously vindictive woman. If she were in charge, she'd tell this Cat Cotter to leave and not come back.

CHAPTER 9

Chief Raleigh had been on the job only two weeks, so when he answered Astrid's call, she stammered in surprise.

"I…I'm Astrid Lincoln at *The Bugle*," she said. "I expected a clerk to answer, Chief Raleigh. We've had a report of a bank robbery in town. The City Bank, we were told."

"Huh. That's funny. Where did your informant get that?"

"You mean there hasn't been a robbery?"

"Not that I know about. Why did someone think that?"

"She said she saw two small men in Halloween masks running in front of the bank."

"I know what she saw." He laughed. "My kid is one of them. They were having a scavenger hunt for a school project. The bank was contacted before they went there. It's a project to help the family that burned out last week. She probably saw their sacks and costumes and thought they were carrying out money. The tellers brought clothes to be donated. We'll check it out, but I think there has been no robbery today."

When Astrid hung up, she could feel the color rising in her face. Did *that* sound familiar. She wouldn't speak of her own misadventure in a similar situation, but she hastily told Dee what Cat's bank robbery was all about.

"Oh, dear. And I sent Charlie off with a camera. That woman. I could kick myself for believing her. She seems to be nothing but trouble."

"That's what I think, Dee. What I'd like to know is how come she's here in Fairchance."

"Apparently she and her husband kept their house here, even though they both worked in the Boston area for a while. Then they retired and came back to live. She wants a job, even though she's 72. Said she didn't want to go back to teaching."

"Teaching?" Astrid couldn't help but sound incredulous. "Imagine having her for a teacher?"

"Yeah. Charlie and I said that, too. But I thought from her newspaper clippings that she would be a good reporter. I don't know. I feel sorry for her. You know, she may be capable of turning in good stories. Maybe this militia group is just a misunderstanding. Or it's possible, I suppose, that she's right, too. They may be up to no good."

"For a school teacher and a newspaper reporter, she acts more like your everyday next-door gossip who would like nothing better than to destroy a reputation and spread misery any way she can."

"It does appear that way. Well, when Charlie can get out there, we'll find out. I don't think he'll be in any danger. According to Sheriff Knight, they aren't outside the law, just a group of people who happen to enjoy guns. Not too unusual in Maine."

"No. I used to hunt years ago as a teenager. We all did in the family. All but my mother. She wasn't very strong."

"What did you hunt? Birds? Deer?"

"All of it. Our freezer was always full of meat, wild and farm-raised."

"I never went hunting myself. Don't really like guns. You must be a good shot then."

Astrid shrugged.

"I have a couple of marksmanship trophies."

She never boasted about her superior marksmanship awards and felt embarrassed to speak of the trophies. In fact, she only took part in the shooting contests to prove to an overbearing young man that she was as good as he was just to shut him up about his successes on the shooting range. Thankfully, Dee didn't ask more questions, and that ended the possibility of sounding as puffed up as he was.

They both returned to their work, but Astrid continued to think about Cat Cotter and her ongoing crusade. It had been several years since she was fired from her job at the *Christian Science Monitor* for writing scathing columns and sending them out under the false heading of CSM syndicated. Could she be a harmful woman, more so than merely spreading what appeared to be false accusations? As Dee pointed out, the possibility that the woods camp presented a real threat to society was something to be weighed before passing condemnation on Cat. Astrid, however, believed reputation spoke for itself. They could expect nothing more than confusion and continued interruption from Cat Cotter. How much damage she might do remained to be seen.

"Well, there wasn't any bank robbery," Charlie said at the doorway. "But it wasn't a wasted trip. I took a few good photos of a scavenger hunt going on."

He had tongue in cheek.

"Ya. We heard."

He hesitated where he stood wearing a look that said *might have known* before telling Dee, "Here's some mail. I went to the Post Office while I was downtown."

"Thanks." She reached for the stack of envelopes and held them for a moment before saying, "Tell you what, Charlie. This is your job now. Go ahead and open the mail. You know all about distributing it."

Taking it all back, he said, "I know the best place for most of it to go, but I'll see that it's shared…without prejudice."

"You're too good."

Charlie opened mostly correspondents' mail until he came to one that he held to his nose and sniffed.

"Nice perfume," he said. "Must be a fan letter to me. Hello. About time. Dee, you've got an application. And I would hazard a guess that it's from a woman."

"I've been hoping for more applications. Let me see."

As she read it, Charlie said, "Well, well. Seems like today's your lucky day, Dee. Here's another one. This is a man."

"And I was worried that I'd have to hire Cat Cotter."

Charlie and Astrid groaned in unison.

"I can just see the office with Cat here." Charlie said. "We'd all be so worn out at the end of the day after her chatter that we'd drag home and fall asleep on the couch every evening. I don't think Jenny would be too pleased with that outcome."

"Nor Abram. Either one of them look like a good prospect, Dee?"

"Both look quite good. Listen to this one. She's a University of Maine graduate. She enjoys theater, dancing, cooking, and writing poetry. She had high grades in journalism. But she doesn't list previous experience, so she may be just out of college."

"We could have a poet's corner."

"I think not, Charlie. This other one was graduated from a two-year college in New York State, and sounds a bit older since he has a bundle of experience and is married. He worked as a part-time political reporter, edited an agricultural newsletter as well as a newsletter for an historical society. He was a sports reporter for the Binghamton Press."

Astrid considered those qualifications before asking, "Wonder why he wants to come here? Does he say?"

"No. But that's a good question to ask when we interview him. I'll put these in your hands, Charlie, and you can call both to see when they might come for an interview. Let's hope it will be soon."

"You're anxious to go upstairs?" Astrid said.

"In a way. I want to go over the duties more carefully with Marvin, now that he's back all rested and ready to work. He's relieved not to continue as publisher. As yet, I've had no definitive work outline from him. I know there's a good deal more than just attending dinner parties to garner advertising. Actually, he didn't do much of that himself."

"Will you be reporting at all?" Astrid asked.

"Don't know that yet. I've told Charlie that I'll keep my hand in by writing the occasional editorial. We'll have to work that out, too."

Astrid could wait no longer.

"Dee, I know you plan to have Charlie go out to that militia camp, but do you think that's the best use of his time? I mean, here you plan to have him interview candidates and he needs to move to his new home from Twin Ports. It seems to me that I would be the better choice for checking out The Kingdom camp. Since the sheriff has said that they are not lawbreakers, then I should be perfectly able to do the assignment without risk. What do you think?"

"Oh. I don't know. I only thought that a man might be more…"

"What? More aggressive? I can be that."

Dee and Charlie both grinned.

"Of course," Dee said. "You're right. But if it looks like trouble, I don't want you hanging around. Understood?"

"Okay." Astrid felt pressure on her little finger coming from the wedding ring, and adjusted it. "I can go tomorrow. You see? Charlie wouldn't be ready to go that soon. Everything will be just fine."

CHAPTER 10

Astrid couldn't wait to tell Abram all that went on this day. She felt almost giddy with excitement as she parked her Jeep in the garage. It was just so damn good to be back at work and to have an adventure ahead of her at the camp that Cat Cotter termed a KKK site. Ridiculous. What she'd find, no doubt, would be a group of people down on their luck. Maybe she'd be able to help them out a bit with a cash donation. To say the least, she could write an article about their conditions, being careful not to sound lofty, and she would try to inspire a feeling of good will and generosity among townspeople, rather than fear and vitriol that Cat seemed bent on spreading.

She came from the garage through the kitchen door and yelled Abram's name.

"I'm in here, Astrid."

His voice sounded weak. Astrid hurried into the den only to find him lying on the sofa, pale and shivering beneath an afghan.

"What's wrong, Abram? Are you sick?"

"You could say that. All of a sudden this afternoon I began to feel dizzy. I guess the honeymoon was too much for me."

He gave her a sly look, but she didn't find it amusing, given that he was hoarse and looked drained.

"You must have a cold, or maybe bronchitis, or flu. I'll take you to the emergency room."

"No," he said, holding out his hand to stop her. "I just need to rest, I think."

"Oh Abram. I'm so sorry that you're ill. Tell you what. I'll do what my grandfather always did for me when I came down with a cold. I'll make some chicken soup."

"Please. Don't. You don't have any chicken. Besides, I don't like chicken soup. I really don't want to eat. You go ahead and have your own supper. I just want to rest."

"I'll bring you some hot broth, at least. And I'd better call the sheriff and tell him. They're expecting you to work tomorrow."

"Maybe I'll be better tomorrow."

The effort of talking set off a coughing spasm.

"I doubt that. Better to call in right now than to wait until tomorrow."

"Whatever."

For Abram not to give her an argument signified how ill he was. Now came the question of whether to go out to The Kingdom tomorrow. She couldn't leave him like this. If he was no better by morning, she'd get him to the doctor for an antibiotic, or whatever he needed. He was her priority.

She wasn't quite out the door on her way to the kitchen when she heard Abram mumble, "Damned ring."

It wasn't the first time he had said that, though he seemed to think she couldn't hear, and she still didn't know what he was talking about. However, this was no time to confront him about anything. Someday, when he felt better, they could discuss whatever he meant. It seemed to be more than just a little thing. It seemed to be a form of cursing from the way he threw a hand over his eyes. She had noticed that gesture before, too. What could be his problem about the ring? Did he literally mean the ring, or was there a more sinister meaning to his regret…like maybe he was sorry that he married her?

"Stop it," she told herself as she put a TV dinner in the microwave. "You're not the problem or he wouldn't hesitate to tell you."

But the ring. She held up her left hand and ran a finger over the shining gems. So beautiful. Why did it agitate him? It couldn't be that he stole it. She wouldn't even consider that. He said it was inherited from a great aunt. Did he feel guilty about having lived off her money while he recuperated from the shoulder operation, all the while in possession of this ring that could have brought him a lot of money? That seemed far-fetched, too.

Oh well, she'd get the answers some day, but not now. Time to call the sheriff.

The clerk who answered said the sheriff was not at the office. Astrid hung up and dialed his home phone number

"Hello." Beth's soft voice reminded Astrid that she needed to work still harder on toning down her own volume.

"Beth, this is Astrid Lincoln. I apologize for calling your home phone, but I need to talk with Larry if he's not busy."

Beth called out Larry's name, then she said, "You're back from your honeymoon so soon, Astrid?"

"It's a long story. But yes, we decided to come back early. I was needed at the office."

"I know how that is. Too bad, though, that you had to cut your honeymoon short. Did you take the cruise?"

"No. The weather was too cold and windy. We decided to do it another time."

"That's understandable. You want to have fun, not be bundled up and miserable when you're on a Caribbean cruise."

"Ya. That's what we thought. And how's that big boy of yours?"

"Getting cuter every day. It's so much fun to watch a baby as he learns new things. You ought to try it, Astrid."

They both laughed and Astrid agreed that she would--some day.

"It's good talking with you. Come visit us any time," Beth said. "Here's Larry now."

A pause, then Larry said, "Astrid. What's wrong?"

"Two things. First, Abram is very ill. I think he has flu and if he's no better tomorrow morning, I'll get him to the doctor. Wanted to let you know that he just can't make it to work."

"Of course not. You take care of him. I'll bring in someone else."

"Thanks. The other thing is that we need to investigate that group out in Greenboro. I say we *need* to--more like we've had a report about them and Dee wants to investigate the situation before residents here get all worked up over it. You know?"

"Right. I can give you what information I have about them if you want to come in tomorrow sometime. That's assuming you can leave Abram."

"If need be, he can be admitted to the hospital. But I feel quite sure I'll be able to work part of the day anyway. How about I go to your office in the afternoon? What time would work for you?"

"Say about 2 o'clock?"

"Okay. I'll be there."

"And Astrid, are you planning to go to the camp by your-self?"

"Ya. I'll go out. We're short-handed, now that Natalie is gone."

"She'll be missed. What I want to say is you should be very careful. I don't know that they are troublesome, but given the nature of their pastime, I'd say you can't be too careful. You ought to have someone with you. I can't spare a deputy. The flu has run through my department and we're short-handed, too. So don't take any chances. If it looks like trouble in any way, get out of there. Understood?"

"Ya. Understood. I'm sure the report we've received has been greatly exaggerated. If that's the case, then we're obligated to let our readers know the truth. Gossip will only inflame people, as you know."

"Uh, huh, I know. I'll see you tomorrow. Tell Abram not to come in until he's fully recovered."

The microwave was intermittently dinging for her attention when she hung up. Astrid missed the restaurant meals they enjoyed in Florida, but for now this would do. Some day she'd get serious about actually cooking. It wasn't that she couldn't cook. She just didn't like to. But some things had to be done whether one liked to or not, like confronting a gang of gun-toting people out in the woods and hoping they were friendly. Just like a western movie. Would the unknown natives be friendly? Or would they circle the town and burn the wagons?

"Silly thought."

Still, after reading the story that Cat Cotter wrote, one had to consider the possibility that they could be planning mayhem, as unlikely as it seemed.

She wanted to believe that nothing would happen, that it would all turn out to be just the wild imagination of a rather flighty old woman with nothing to do but create a fantasy story in her mind.

And yet…No. It can't be. I won't worry one bit. I'll just go out there, shake hands, talk with a few people, and write a nice piece about this group who decided to band together in order to live more comfortably than on the street. Easy. Piece of cake. No problem.

As she passed the hallway mirror to go upstairs, she glanced at her reflection. Despite shrugging off the upcoming assignment, there was no denying the taut facial lines. She opened her eyes wide and pulled herself up straight. It wasn't too long ago that she had faced a gun in the hands of a known killer, and that was something she definitely did not want to repeat.

Now that she thought about it, no doubt it would be best not to tell Abram about this plan of going alone to a woods camp where there were guns, where faces reflected suspicion and distrust, if you could believe Cat Cotter. Would they greet her with weapons in hand? She tamped down a shudder, set her jaw, and ran up the stairs to change into evening leisure clothes. Her heart beat faster to the rhythm of the words "Don't take chances. Don't take chances."

Of course I won't take chances. I know how to take care of myself. You think I'd just rush into an unknown situation without being extra careful? As if I'd leap into danger head first. No one can possibly think I'm that naive.

CHAPTER 11

Dee cleared her desk, ready to leave for her meeting with Marvin. She'd like to remind Charlie to straighten up his desk, but said nothing, having told him early on that she liked to have desks neat and tidy when they left the office for the night. He maintained that everything on his desk should remain where it was. If he (or anyone else) started picking up the papers for the sake of appearance, he wouldn't be able to find anything. And it did appear that it worked for him, since he could always come up with what was needed.

"How's Jenny coming with the packing?" Dee asked. "She ready for the big move, do you think? She's a real home body."

"She's surprisingly calm about it, even seems excited about beginning a new life here. I never would have expected her to cope so well."

"She has that certain something that seems to roll with whatever life throws at her. I've seen it before. It's a great quality, and what we all love about her."

Charlie grinned from ear to ear. "Yeah. You've got that right."

"And how about you, Charlie? Are you happy with making this change?"

Dee did think Jenny would get along well with this town. Would Charlie? As yet, he didn't seem very enthused about the editor's position. Of course, when Jen got here and they were in their rental, he'd likely come to life.

"I'm happy enough," he said. "I've been lonely without Jenny."

"Regarding where I will work," Dee said. "I've decided to move upstairs after we get the new reporter. You'll have more control. The only thing is that I'm not sure I won't get lonely up there. May want to make different arrangements, but we'll wait and see how it works out."

"I hope you don't think your presence here is a problem with me. You'll always have the final say, no matter where your desk is. There's nothing wrong with this arrangement as far as I'm concerned."

It was gracious of him to say that, but Dee knew better.

"I appreciate that. However, the publisher's office has always been upstairs, even though Marvin didn't use it much. I think it will be just fine."

"You're going to see Mr. Cornell now?" he asked.

"It's about that time."

"I wanted to ask you something, if you can take an extra few minutes."

"Sure. Shoot."

"Astrid is an excellent worker and a good reporter. Don't you agree?"

"She's all that."

"I know the newspaper is small, and has never given a special editorial title to the other reporter, but I was just wondering if you would consider giving her a promotion to news editor. She could move to your desk and leave hers for the new reporter. So there'd be me as editor, Astrid as news editor, and whoever we hire as sports editor."

"A title for everyone," Dee said. "She hasn't been here long. Nor have I, for that matter, but I see no reason why she shouldn't move up a notch. We'll discuss it more tomorrow after we interview the candidate. That's right, isn't it? Just one candidate?"

Charlie nodded.

"Willis Boxer. As it turns out, the telephone number he listed is that of his parents, who now live in Camden. That's why he's trying to get a job in Maine. He'll be here at 10 a.m. I couldn't reach the woman. Let's see," he looked at the resume, "here it is. Her name is Anne Ryan. She lives in Ellsworth, so if I can reach her early this evening, I'll see if she can come in tomorrow, too. If we can talk with both, maybe we can get the new reporter soon."

"You're right. We need someone very soon. Now, I have to go. See you tomorrow."

"You bet."

Dee pulled her coat collar up when she reached the back parking lot to walk over to Marvin's office. As soon as the sun faded, the temperature dropped, and it felt like it might be in the teens already.

Marvin was waiting for her at the door, and opened it for her.

"Come in, Dee. Get out of the cold wind. I guess it will be close to zero by morning."

"Feels like it now. The lawyer here?"

"In my office. He just got here."

Attorney Johnson stood up when the two of them walked into the office. He held out his hand to Dee.

"Hi," he said so informally that Dee wondered if she had met him before, but he had not been present for the document signing. "I'm Jeremiah Johnson. Call me J.J. My parents liked Biblical names. They named my sister Ruth and my brothers,

81

Matthew and Luke. If they hoped their children would walk the straight and narrow path of righteousness, they have been terribly disappointed."

Dee laughed. "Why is that? I can understand why a lawyer might not fit the bill. What about the others?"

"Oh, well, Ruth became a corporate attorney, Matthew is a singer and usually unemployed, and Luke writes science fiction and is all but starving in his girlfriend's New York City apartment. How's that for worldliness?"

Again everyone laughed as they sat next to the desk, ready for the task at hand. If Marvin had opened a box of thousand dollar bills, he couldn't have glowed more. Dee liked that. It had been a long period of adjustment for him. Now he was ready to let go and embrace the future.

J.J. was another matter. Dee couldn't determine if he was just a very happy man, or a tricky one. Her own attorney in Twin Ports never gave her cause for worry, but there was something ingenuous about this one. His piercing eyes said he shouldn't be taken at face value. He wouldn't break, but he would quickly break another person, Dee thought. Probably relentless in the court room, and she hoped she'd never have to experience that detail about him.

"Okay, my friends, we're ready to make this deal all legal, signed, sealed, and delivered. Marvin, I've placed an x where you need to initial the agreement. And Dee, you can initial on the lines next to each of his. Just a small detail that my secretary overlooked when you signed before."

His secretary was a soft spoken young woman whose hands had shook when she talked with Marvin and Dee. If she was that nervous, what would she do when confronted with an error like missing two almost invisible places for initials? Dee could imagine the flow of tears, the plea for forgiveness. Would she be forgiven, or would the poor woman lose her position? Dee had her suspicions.

Finished, J.J. stood up, tucked the paperwork into a large leather briefcase, and said, "All right. That wraps it up. Congratulations, Dee, you now own this rag that Marvin calls a newspaper."

He laughed, Marvin smiled, but Dee held her chin high and said, "This newspaper is a proud member of the community of Fairchance. I hope you can boast the same, J.J. "

"Just joking, my dear. Of course it is. My week wouldn't be complete without the news of Fairchance and surrounding towns. Like I said, I congratulate you."

You pompous ass, Dee thought. She realized that thought was more like an Astrid remark than hers. Nevertheless, he couldn't be more pedantic if he had gone into the ministry to please his parents.

After Marvin and Dee saw him off at the door, they both returned to the office and sat side-by-side on the sofa beneath a bay window that looked out on the parking lot, *The Bugle* office building, and Main Street.

"You know, Marvin, I really don't trust that man. Are you sure he's the best you could have for a lawyer?"

"He's okay. An old friend of the family. If there's a real legal problem, he's the lawyer you want on your side, believe me."

They both stared out the window for minutes before Marvin spoke again.

"Is everything going all right, Dee? You've been without a full staff. Have you been able to cope okay?"

"Thank you for asking. It's been hard. But Charlie is so capable that we've been able to manage. He came up with the thought of promoting Astrid to news editor. Odd that the title hasn't been created before now."

Marvin nodded in approval.

"It is at that. And what are you planning to do? Stay on in editorial as publisher/editor?"

"Oh no. Charlie is the editor. I'll go up to the publisher's office and write whatever I need to there."

"If I'd had more interest in the news end of the business, I'd have been there more, and I'd probably have had the business manager in the next room. He'd provide company as well as daily hands-on to the financial end of the business. You might consider that, and maybe he should share an office with the ad manager."

"Excellent ideas. I'll give it serious consideration. Right now, I'll be happy to get all the slots filled in editorial. We're interviewing at least one candidate tomorrow morning."

"For sports. Yes. You want to have all the reporters you can, but remember that employees create the bulk of expenditure for any company. I don't have to tell you. It's just a reminder not to overload."

"I hadn't really thought of more staff. Three good reporters can handle it all just fine. And I'm always available to fill in."

To her surprise, Marvin reached over and took her hand, held it in both of his.

"I have faith in your ability to do the job, Dee. So I hope you won't lose heart at any time. If you do feel overwhelmed, I'm always here, just across the parking lot. My door is always open, and I'll be happy to help in any way I can, if it's no more than moral support."

His grip was firm, and his eyes were so warm they seemed to plead for closer contact. Dee felt a yearning that she hadn't experienced in many years. Marvin was a good man, but more than that, the two of them had shared similar emotional conflict, which most individuals would not expect until a much older age. Though they said little of the tragic deaths of her husband so many years ago and of his wife only in the past several weeks, their losses forged a bond between them.

Feeling giddy, she knew that if she didn't want to embarrass herself, she needed to conclude this interlude.

"I do appreciate your support, Marvin. I won't forget about your open door. I'm sure I will have many questions as I get into this business."

She withdrew her hand from his and stood up to go, went to the chair where she had left her coat.

Marvin followed her, and though she was back to him, she could feel his eyes still pulling her. She went to the door, but he was there first, resting his hand on the doorknob.

"Dee." She detected breathlessness. "You've always intrigued me, you know. I don't want to be pushy, but…well…could we see a bit more of each other? Maybe you'd have dinner with me tomorrow? I could pick you up at 6:30, if you'd care to join me."

She went numb all over. His interest had been apparent, and she knew it. But, all the same, for him to come right out and say it was unexpected. She told herself not to start shaking, stay calm, meet his eyes.

"That would be very nice, Marvin. I'll be ready at 6:30."

"Good. It's a date, then."

Outside, the cold air set Dee's teeth chattering. Her knees felt like they would buckle.

Take it easy, old gal, she told herself. *It's just a dinner date, after all. It's not as if he's asking you to marry him, or anything. Seeing each other a bit more often would be nice. And that's all there is to it. Don't act like a jerk.*

. . . .

After a night of coughing, Abram had a high fever, and Astrid wasted no time calling the doctor again to tell him. She was told to bundle him up and take him to the hospital where they would be waiting to admit him immediately.

Once again she found herself in the lobby outside his hospital room. This was the third hospitalization for him in recent months. Silently, she prayed it would not be too serious, and that it would be his last time here in a very long time. He wasn't accident prone, just seemed to have poor luck.

She twisted the wedding ring on her finger and recalled the times that she had heard him say, "Damned ring." Not knowing why, she began to feel that it had something to do with the mishaps they were experiencing, but dismissed the thought as worse than frivolous. *Just damned stupid.*

It was obvious that she couldn't go to the militia camp today. She went to the desk and asked to use a phone. The woman who answered in the business office asked her to wait a minute, and then Dee came on the line.

"Dee, I'm at the hospital with Abram. He's very ill with what the doctor says is flu. I don't want to leave him for long, so I won't be able to go to Greenboro, at least not today."

"No, of course not, Astrid. You stay with him today, and don't plan to go to Greenboro until next week. There's really no great urgency to follow up on this story. Perhaps Monday when you're life is more settled will be the best time to go. Charlie and his wife are moving here this weekend, and things are all up in the air at the moment. I'll help Jenny settle in. If you need tomorrow, take it off, too, and we'll see you Monday, hopefully."

Astrid thanked her and hung up with relief. Now all her attention could go to getting her husband well.

CHAPTER 12

Roy Cotter feared the signs. Maybe it was time to take Cat to the doctor and explain how she was acting, how she had gone on this tangent before and was diagnosed then as displaying signs of bipolar personality. Even though medication helped at the time, he never thought she was bipolar. Her erratic behavior started after her younger brother was killed in Boston. To Roy, the problem was her obsession with trying to exact justice for that shooting, even though no one knew who the drive-by shooter was. By weapons association, militia groups filled that bill for Cat. She seemed to think that they all should be eradicated. She fantasized about their danger to society, even tried to stir up nationwide sympathy for her cause by sending out huge mailings of columns she wrote, until she was caught by her employers and warned never to use the newspaper's name again. The experience of losing her position plunged her into deep depression for about a month.

Bringing her back to Maine seemed like the solution. Surely she would forget her crusade, he thought. But since James Kinsley talked about the group he encountered in Greenboro…a group of gun-toting misfits he called them…she talked incessantly about this militia group's getting ready to attack innocent citizens right here in Fairchance.

He watched her now, frantically pounding away on her portable typewriter, looking up only to check through her pile of notes that she had been scribbling for years or picking up her scrapbook of newspaper clippings, a collection made since Bernie's death. This had to stop. They couldn't go on like this. It was driving both of them crazy.

"Cat," he said, putting down his book. "isn't it time you left your project for the night?"

"I'm not finished yet. You go up to bed if you want. I'll just work a while longer."

"You've been working at it all afternoon. You should give it a rest."

"I'll never rest. This has to be done."

"But it's Saturday night, my dear. Saturday night, you know."

She looked up just long enough to say, "I know that. We'll just have to wait until tomorrow night."

"Cat, I don't want you to work any longer. We can wait, if you wish, but I insist that you stop typing for the night."

"You insist?" With just two words, she could wound as sharply as if she'd thrown a knife. "Well I insist that I finish this. It's important. You don't understand."

Usually he would quietly leave when she jabbed at him, but this was going too far. He was losing patience. He walked to her side, grabbed the paper she was typing and pulled it from the machine.

"What are you doing? You'll ruin my letter."

"Exactly. And if you don't stop this right now, I'll throw all that stuff you've been doing into the fire. Now I said it's time to go to bed. Next week I'm taking you to the doctor to get the medication you need. You're acting like a mad woman, and I know you're not mad. "

"What do you know about anything?" Her question was uncharacteristic. "How could you forget so soon? I can't forget the sight of him in the coroner's office, lifeless. I'd give anything to bring him back."

She burst into a jagged sob. Roy pulled her to her feet, put his arm around her, and guided her to the stairs. She still felt like a child to him, just like she had when he married her.

"But you can't bring your brother back, my dear. You must accept that fact. Why don't you ask his family to come here for a few weeks?"

"His family? I hope you don't mean that woman who was so in love with him that she married the first man who smiled at her after he died. His children are both too far away and probably don't give a hoot about their old aunt. They never write. No one cares any more."

"They care, but they have their own lives to live. And we do, too. You don't know who shot Bernie. Police don't know. It's unfair to judge a group who had nothing to do with it. It's not like you to be unfair."

He hoped those last words would cut through her fog. Apparently they did. She looked up and said, "Well, why are we arguing? Let's get upstairs where we belong on a Saturday evening."

Life with Cat had been on a see-saw of late and Roy felt like he was on the brink of a breakdown himself. When he looked back at how it was before that dreadful shooting in Boston when her brother dropped dead on the sidewalk, he couldn't find much these days that compared with it. Sometimes he thought that if they hadn't gone there so that she could see him more often, it wouldn't have been so traumatic for her. The worst of it was that Bernie was on his way from his home in Waltham to visit them, and that made her feel guilty. On the other hand, no matter where they lived, she'd have felt like she had lost her own child. She had been a second mother to him as he grew up, being 15 years his senior with no other siblings. Since she could never have children of her own, she continued to look on him as her responsibility, even after he was married and had two children.

For now, Roy must focus on bringing her back to normal and somehow he needed to convince her to give up this nonsense about the danger of a ragtag group out in the woods.

· · · ·

Astrid had reached the door when the phone rang. Not wanting Abram to wake up, she ran back to answer it in the kitchen.

"How is Abram?" Dee asked without preamble.

"He's better. The doctor said he has 24-hour flu and will be okay. I was just going out the door when you called."

"Good. We're interviewing a candidate at ten. Charlie isn't here yet, so I'm not sure about the other one who applied. He was going to call her last evening. I was hoping you'd be here, too."

"Ya. I'll be there in about 15 minutes. I'll bring sweet rolls."

"Are you planning to go to Greenboro today?"

"I was, but then I decided to wait until Monday, or if you can't spare me then, maybe Wednesday morning. I haven't said anything to Abram about it yet."

"Wednesday would be better. Charlie and Jenny are moving here this weekend. He may not be in early Monday."

"Ya. He'll have a lot to do just settling in. See you soon."

She stopped at the supermarket on the way. It was handy for her, but she missed stopping at the Main Street Bakery for their fresh baked goods. Some morning, when she had more time, she'd scoot out to the bakery and chat for a few minutes with Sonny, like she did when she was living at the motel. *Too bad one of his kids won't take over the bakery,* she thought.

From the supermarket it was only minutes to *The Bugle* office, a pretty, remodeled Cape situated on the hillside bend in Main Street. It was an ideal place to be, overlooking the hub of the small, but active, city. Astrid found herself more and more in love with this place as time went on, and she entered the office suddenly full of pride that her work was meaningful and her place of business was charming.

"Hi, Dee," she said. "Charlie not here yet?"

"He's coming. Just called in. He said our young woman, Anne Ryan, will be coming for the interview, also. He scheduled her at 11. I'm not sure about her qualifications, even though she's a journalism graduate. Sometimes they don't make the best reporters."

Not only did Astrid wonder how Dee would know that, she also felt a tiny bit of resentment, being a journalism graduate herself. Dee's early background was pretty much a mystery to Astrid. Where she went to college, where she worked in a newspaper office, how she advanced so quickly to the publisher's chair.

"Astrid," Dee continued, "there's something I need to tell you. I've decided to use the office upstairs, and I'll probably have the business manager Jeremy join me there. Charlie, of course, will have Natalie's old place, as he already has. As for you, we're advancing you to the title of news editor, and you will occupy this desk. The new reporter will be sports editor, although I've been thinking we might want to change that to reporter at large, since duties vary so much. There will be a raise for you of $2,000 annually for now."

Astrid had walked in with pride swelling in her chest. Now she felt like she'd burst. Her grandfather had left her wealthy enough that she never needed to work for a living, but it was what she liked to do. The only other option, as far as she was concerned, was to operate a farm, and for now she was happy here.

"Well, I'm honored," was all she could say. "Thank you."

"This is a small newspaper, to be sure, but we do a whole lot more than most publications this size, and you're a large part of making it so. I came here with more years out of the news gathering business than in it, but what training I had beyond college, was top rate at a similar newspaper in Westburgh, New York. I feel that you've had a superior learning experience, and I know that the three of you, with my occasional contribution, will make this newspaper grow."

"We'll all try," Astrid said. "When did you work at that newspaper?"

"Years ago. I was there for a year, but returned to Twin Ports at my mother's request."

She hesitated, obviously suddenly emotional. When she composed herself, she continued.

"When I got home, the police told me she had committed suicide. I knew she'd never do that, not ever, but especially not when she knew I was coming home. Well, it turned out I was right. She had been murdered. After the ordeal of proving it, I then married Barry Poore and developed the rehab camp, to honor my mother's wishes. I ran it for close to ten years. Natalie and I met by chance at a Fairchance College conference and renewed our long-ago friendship. I had just closed the rehab camp, and she asked me to join her here. Now look at me. I never in the world expected to own a newspaper."

She said, "Natalie and I..." but was interrupted when Charlie came in, looking exhausted.

"My god, Charlie," Astrid blurted. "You look like hell."

She glanced at Dee to see any reaction to her language. She had been careful to talk less like a rough farmer and more like what everyone called a lady, and most of the time controlled it these days.

Dee showed only concern for Charlie.

"You okay?" she asked.

"Yeah. A bit tired. I went to Twin Ports to help Jen last night. It was a mad house. I got a few things done for her and promised to go back tonight."

"You should have called me," Dee said. "You didn't really need to come in today."

"Well, I've set up two interviews. I thought I should be here. After all, I *am* the editor."

For a second, Astrid thought he and Dee might exchange sharp words over his emphasis on that fact. Dee's face went blank and she lowered her eyes, no doubt telling herself to cool it. She had once told Astrid that Charlie had a sharp temper, but always got over it quickly.

When Dee looked at Charlie again, she gave him a crooked smile, nodded, and said, "You're right. After we do this, go home. Jen obviously needs you. In the meantime, there's food in the lounge. Take a few minutes to eat, have some coffee. And for goodness sake, comb your hair."

Well, she got in a dig after all. Astrid noted that Charlie said nothing to that, but did go to the lounge. She fully expected that he would collapse onto the sofa and grab a few winks.

Her mind wandered to her own upcoming assignment in Greenboro, and the more she thought about it, the more it loomed as an insurmountable task. Perhaps the encounter with real killers just a couple months ago shook her confidence more than she ever let anyone know. On the other hand, it was uncertain if those camped out there were killers. Very likely they weren't. So why did she feel apprehensive?

CHAPTER 13

Willis Boxer arrived 15 minutes early, in a well-worn black suit, black turtleneck sweater, and cracked, but polished, black shoes. The outside temperature had warmed, but still registered less than 20 degrees. He must be cold without an overcoat, Astrid thought. However, closer scrutiny revealed weathered, tan skin as well as blond hair that looked white in a ray of sunshine, signs of a love for the outdoors.

"Hello," he said, "I'm here for an interview. Willis Boxer."

Dee rose quickly and went to shake his hand.

"Glad to meet you, Willis. This is Astrid Thor…rather, Lincoln now that she's married." She turned to Astrid and said, "Go get Charlie, please."

"I hope I'm not too early."

"No, no. The editor will be here in a second. He's just getting himself coffee in the lounge."

As Astrid expected, Charlie had gone asleep on the sofa. She hated to wake him, but shook him gently.

"Wha…? Oh, Astrid. What's up? Is Willis here?"

"Ya. He just came in. Here," she reached in a drawer that held several cosmetic items, "use this comb to push your hair back a bit."

He raked the comb through his collar-length hair, but when he handed it back to her she shook her head.

"Didn't make much difference, I guess," she said.

"What's he like?"

Astrid had noticed that Charlie often ignored references to his shaggy appearance. Whether he didn't care or just wanted to express independence, she hadn't determined yet.

"He looks nervous. Good looking, though."

"Okay. I'll be in. Just give me a few minutes."

She returned. "Charlie will be right in. He's finishing his coffee."

Then she thought to ask, "Would you like coffee, Willis?"

"Everyone calls me Will. No thanks. I don't drink coffee."

Should have known, Astrid thought. All-American athlete, and all that.

"My grandfather used to say that they should have let me drink coffee when I was eight years old. Maybe it would have kept me from growing so tall."

"Well," Dee said, "look at it this way. At least you don't have to stand on a chair to change a light bulb."

Will laughed with the others, and his face muscles relaxed.

"Who's changing light bulbs?" Charlie said on entering.

"We're just saying Astrid doesn't need to stand on a chair to change one," Dee said. "Charlie, this is Will Boxer. Will, you've already talked with our editor, Charlie Hart."

"Yes." Will held out his hand. "Good to meet you in person."

Will took the chair offered, beside Charlie's desk. Astrid rolled her chair to Dee's desk. She noticed the instant rapport between the two men, a good sign.

Charlie take the lead.

"Okay, Will. First of all, sports are big here. We have an active high school sports program--basketball, football, baseball, soccer for inter-scholastic matches. The girls have basketball and soccer. They have intramurals. Tennis is big with girls. Most area schools don't have tennis. At Fairchance College, the attraction is football, but they have all the rest. Women excel in basketball and soccer. They have a new ice arena and plan to introduce hockey. It hasn't really caught on yet."

"I'm familiar with all those sports," Will said. "I like hockey, too. I've had three teeth replaced because of that sport. Is there a chess club at one of the schools?"

"I can answer that," Astrid said. "There is no chess club, but there should be. You like chess, then?"

"My wife and I both play. Friends of ours used to come over for chess. Sometimes we had three games going at a time."

Astrid said no more, but thought that it was a great idea. She'd speak of it to Abram.

"Maybe if the school had a leader for a club, it could be started," Dee offered.

"Actually someone needs to start a teen club for things like chess, other table games," Charlie said. "Dancing, too. If you propose it at a school board meeting, they might approve it. Just remember. If you suggest it, you lead it."

"I understand that, believe me," Will said. "Happened to me before."

Astrid had noticed in the past that the first five minutes of an interview generally were enough to determine whether the candidate would fill the position or not. In this case, she felt sure Will had it. He was self-confident, and he knew sports. She liked his resume and his enthusiasm.

Dee thumbed through his application and work samples.

"I see that you have reported on a variety of subjects. Are you more interested in one type of reporting than in others?"

"No. I like sports, obviously. But I will take any assignment and do my best to have a complete and accurate report to turn in."

"Sometimes," Charlie said, "we get a last-minute call...maybe an accident or a fire, or robbery...and getting the information, writing it up, and having it ready for deadline can be a challenge. Do you have experience with emergencies and speed writing?"

"It has never been a problem for me, though I may not write quite as smoothly as if I had an hour or two to write and edit properly. Is that a problem here?"

Good for you, Astrid thought. Find out the expectations.

"No. We all have the same problem."

Dee said, "What about your wife and family? Do they want to come to Fairchance?"

Will cleared his throat as if giving himself time to think.

"Yes. They will cope just fine."

"You have two children?" Astrid asked.

"That's right. Travis is 11 and Julia is eight. Geena, my wife, has a nursing degree. I expect she'd apply to the local hospital for work."

Astrid could address that. "They always need help at the hospital."

When the interview was concluded, Charlie told Will that he would call within 24 hours and asked how long it would take before he could start work.

"Not long. Monday soon enough?"

"Couldn't get much sooner that."

"I thank you all for considering me for the position," Will said at the door. "Mrs. Poore, Mrs. Lincoln..."

"I'm just Charlie. We operate on a first-name basis here."

"Thank you, Charlie."

As the sound of his footsteps faded down the hallway, Charlie turned to Dee.

"I think he'd be a good choice."

"Looks like," she said. "But our other candidate will be here very soon. We might like her better, you know."

"Ya," Astrid said. "We should be fair."

They waited for Anne Ryan to arrive, and she finally did, a half hour late.

Charlie looked her up and down, disapproval written on his face. She might have come from a cocktail party in mink and fur-topped boots, black hair built high atop her head. Astrid couldn't bring herself to take an instant liking to the young woman when she came in and said, "Am I late? So sorry. I saw the cutest outfit in your dress shop downtown and just had to pop in and try it on. But it wasn't me after all."

Her giggle showed an indifference that grated on Astrid. She was certain the others were feeling the same, that this one had little interest in a job.

Dee sat where she was and said, "Come in. You must be Anne Ryan."

"I *am*." She went to Dee's desk. "And who are you?"

"Dee Poore, the publisher. This is Charlie Hart, the editor, and Astrid Lincoln, news editor."

"Hi, all." She waved at each, in turn. "I'll never remember your names. But you can remind me."

Without removing her mink, she sat in the designated chair and moved it so that she faced Charlie.

"The editor. I guess you're the one I talk with, then."

She rolled her eyes in thought before saying, "Well, I assure you I am well qualified for the position here. I am extremely erudite, an A student in college, with honors in English. I have marvelous recommendations from my professors, and a...a com-pendium of character testimonials from friends. Professor Wolford himself asserted his commitment to help me locate the right position for my capabilities. You know, I'm free as the wind, not restricted by a family, so I could actually, you know, represent the paper at any conference you might want to send me to. Well, you know, married people can't always just up and leave their loved ones, now can they? Oh, not that I don't have a loved one or two, but nothing serious. You know. Not yet, anyway."

She patted the back of her hair and giggled.

Astrid looked at Dee whose face reflected the same disgust that she felt.

Charlie measured his words.

"And do you have sample stories you've written, news reports, and the like, you know. Something of your work that we can read, Anne?"

"Oh I have them in the car. What'd you say your name is? You know, I thought you would want to talk with me first. Then, if you liked me and I liked you, I could bring my papers in. My professors praised my work highly. They all thought I was special, you know. Made everyone in my class jealous. "

"College work only?"

"Yes, of course."

"No actual experience at a newspaper?"

"Well, I just graduated, you know."

"I thought you were graduated last year, according to your resume," Dee said.

"Well, you know, it's hard to find a position these days, especially in the area where you want to be. This is near my parents. They have a beautiful old mansion in Ellsworth. Anyways, how could you expect me to have experience yet? I'm looking for a place to start. You have to, you know, give me a chance. I'm sure I can give you anything you want."

She hiked her skirt a half inch over her crossed knees, a move that escaped no one's notice.

"I'm sure," Charlie said with a wry smile. "Okay."

"When do you want me to start then?"

"Oh I'm sorry. Did you think you were hired? Actually, we've made our decision already. Should have told you sooner, but your presentation was so fascinating."

He stood up and walked across the room to open the door.

"You don't want to see my work? I can go get it."

"No. Good luck in your quest for *experience*. I'm sure you'll get it, just not here."

"Well. You could have told me you had someone already, you know. I wasted all this time talking with you."

"Goodbye."

Astrid was the first to say it.

"I think we need an exceptionally, you know, erudite girl with a com-pendium of character testimonials for this office. We could all learn a thing or two."

"I wonder how long it took her to learn that little speech," Dee said. "She should have learned how to pronounce the big words if she was going to use them."

Charlie laughed out loud.

"Boy, I'm slipping. To think I let a pair of legs like that walk out of my life. What was I thinking?"

"Maybe Will has good legs," Dee said.

CHAPTER 14

Abram had gone downstairs before Astrid stirred on Sunday morning. She reached for him in bed only to find his empty pajamas beside her. A quick trip to the bathroom, a robe, slippers, and she was ready to join him.

"You look much better, dear," she said, on entering the kitchen.

He sat reading the Sunday newspaper, so he must have been up for quite a while.

"I feel much better."

"Well, I could have told you that last night," she said. She leaned over and kissed his lips, then wrapped her arms around his shoulders, still holding the kiss.

"More of that and it'll be tomorrow morning before either of us gets out of bed."

"Promises, promises."

She was about to make muffins when she saw that he had set out corn flakes. She reached in the refrigerator for the orange juice instead.

"I'll go to work tomorrow," he said. "I need to call and find out when they want me there. You said several are out sick. Maybe they'll want me in the morning."

Astrid agreed and poured her cereal and milk. She had been contemplating whether to tell him about her assignment to the militia camp. Finally she decided it would be deceitful not to. Besides, now that he was recovered she could see no reason that it would worry him greatly.

"Abram, I need to tell you about an assignment I'll be on this week. There's a woman in town by the name of Cat Cotter. She learned through her neighbor, the funeral director James Kinsley, that there's a group of men and women who appear to be militants camped out near Greenboro. She has been known for trying to incite trouble for similar groups before. No one knows anything about this group, whether they really are dangerous or even if it is a militia camp, but she insists they are dangerous in any case. Larry Knight thinks they are not out to create trouble."

He picked up a section of newspaper and opened it.

"This must be the same woman who wrote a letter to the editor calling for everyone to take up arms, or words to that effect."

Astrid jumped to her feet and went to his side of the table so that she could read the letter over his shoulder.

"Oh my god. Dee told her not to spread this gossip but she's done it. I wonder if Dee has seen it. I'll wait a while before calling her. She may not be up yet."

"Here, take the paper. It looks damaging to me."

Astrid read word-for-word the letter, filled with frightening references to Ku Klux Klan atrocities.

"What is she thinking? Listen to this, Abram. She says, 'People of Maine, have your weapons at the ready. From experience, I know what these men, calling themselves Patriots, are capable of. They will steal, maim, and kill. They are preparing to attack, most likely at night, when you are sleeping. You must take notice...' God in heaven. This woman is out of her mind. I can't wait. I need to call Dee now. Maybe I can go out there today to interview those people before they get attacked. I wonder if Larry Knight has read this. I'll have to call him, too."

"Whoa. Slow down, Dear. It can wait until tomorrow."

"No. I don't think so. We need to start the ball rolling now. If only Charlie weren't moving today. Well, Dee and I will have to handle it."

She waited for six rings and hung up.

"She may have gone to help Charlie and Jenny. Seems like she did indicate that she would help them settle in, and I doubt that they have a phone yet. I don't even know the address."

Astrid dialed Larry Knight, her heart beating faster with each ring, until she had heard seven, and hung up.

"Now what can I do?"

"Nothing. You can wait until tomorrow. Everyone will be working then and…"

"I think I'll just go over to Greenboro now. I can interview as well on a Sunday as a Monday and then we'll have the start of the story for this week."

"Astrid, you're getting yourself all worked up. Don't overreact. I doubt more than a handful of readers would give this letter a second look. Since there has been no news coverage on this, people will just believe that she's a kook."

"Maybe you're right. But I don't think so. I think something needs to be done immediately."

She hadn't wanted to sound angry, but sometimes repressing an emotion was just impossible.

"I'm going upstairs to get dressed," she said.

As she walked out of the room, she heard the words, "Damned ring," whispered, obviously not meant for her ears, but she had sharp hearing, and she knew that was what he said. Why did he keep blasting the ring? She had to find out. But right now a more important question loomed.

What should she do about Cat Cotter's letter to the editor? She felt that the time to do the interview at the camp was right now. If they saw the letter out there, would it incite them to violence? Maybe if she talked with them, she could convince them that Cat was a bit out of her mind, or something.

She was just pulling on her boots when she looked up and saw Abram in the bedroom doorway. His expression gave no clue to what he was thinking, but he soon let her know.

"No, Astrid. I can't let you go out there alone today. It may not be dangerous, but there are guns around, and you don't know the mood of those people. You have to wait. In fact, Larry should send a deputy with you when you go."

"That'd be nice, but he has too few working for anyone to go with me right now. He told me so."

She didn't want to create a scene with her own husband. Anne Ryan's reference to married folks not always being able to go away from home easily came to mind. Young flirt. What did she know? But, as Astrid considered Abram's words and particularly his concern for her safety, she removed her boots.

"Okay, Abram. I'll wait until tomorrow. Maybe Larry will have some men back. If not, I can take one of our men from the advertising department. They're both big and strong and probably would appreciate a day in the field not having to sell advertising. Then, again, maybe it will be worthwhile if the Patriots decide to take out an ad. You never know."

Not funny. She knew that was what he thought. Well, this whole demonstration of power over her wasn't funny, either.

When Abram went back downstairs to finish reading the newspaper, Astrid gave long thought to this condition called marriage. It had its good points, no question about that. But it also presented moments when she'd like to tell her husband to back off. She was able to take care of herself before she met him, and she was quite sure she could still do it. If she weren't married, she'd finish dressing and head out to The Kingdom and have a chat with the group that Cat Cotter thought was out for blood. She believed differently. She believed they were given a bad rap by this one woman, whose own agenda was likely more dangerous than the whole so-called militia put together.

Now she found herself mumbling, "Damned ring," though she was sure her reason for saying it was different from Abram's.

CHAPTER 15

On her way to the office Monday morning, Astrid noticed a group of maybe half a dozen men in front of the Police Station. She had gone this way in order to see Larry at his office, adjacent to the police station. She noticed that one of the men held a folded newspaper and was slapping it with the back of his hand. They all looked angry and the way they were nodding, she suspected they might be discussing Cat's letter to the editor. Tempted to stop and ask, she shrugged it off and drove to the parking lot instead.

It's really not my business. They could be talking sports, maybe tonight's football game on TV, for all I know. I won't stick my nose in.

Larry Knight met her at his office door.

"Astrid. You got here just in time. I was about to leave."

"If you're busy…"

"No, no. Come in. We can talk a few minutes. You're here about the Greenboro camp?"

"Ya. Did you see the letter to the editor that Cat Cotter wrote to the *Bangor Sunday Life?*"

"I did. That's where I was headed, to Mrs. Cotter's home. I need to caution her."

"Good. Have you had any reaction to it here?"

"You saw the men next door?"

Astrid nodded.

"They were here. Now they'll see Chief Raleigh and try to get him to do something, I'm not sure just what. They didn't get a very warm reception from me. I told them the letter was out of line and should be ignored. When there's something to report we'll do it. Reports that we send out are official, not those that come from a citizen. At this time, we don't have a thing, absolutely no reason to run them off that property or out of the state, or to arrest them for. As long as they aren't doing anything illegal, and they're leaving others alone, then we should do the same for them. Leave them alone."

"I'll see if I can get out there today," Astrid said, "so that we can have a more accurate story about their activity in the paper this week. It should calm people down if they know that an attack isn't imminent."

"Good. Anything you need from me?"

"I don't think so. We did speak earlier about having someone go with me on this visit. What do you think?"

"It's advisable, I'd say. But, like I said, I just can't spare anyone from here."

"All right. I think I can get someone from our own office. We'll see. Thank you, Larry. And would you mind letting me know what happens with Cat Cotter?"

"I will do that."

Astrid left, reminding herself that when level heads prevailed, life was much safer. She found Dee already discussing with Will this week's stories. She must have been here a while since the radiator was pouring out heat.

"Good morning," Astrid said. "Good to see you, Will. Is Dee loading you with assignments?"

"Morning," he said. "No, she's being kind to me today."

"It won't last, you know."

"I suspected as much."

Dee jumped in. "If you feel deprived, I can always find more to do."

"She can, too," Astrid said. "Actually I want to request that I go to Greenboro today, Dee. You saw the letter to the editor yesterday?"

"I just read it this morning. I was helping Charlie and Jen get settled yesterday. Yes, I think it's a good idea to get as much as we can right away."

"I stopped to see Larry. Maybe half a dozen men were outside the Police Station, and Larry said they talked with him. It was about that letter. He sent them on their way, told them there was nothing to get excited about. Like he's said all along, as long as the campers aren't breaking the law, he can't do anything. But you can be sure those men aren't the only ones in town worried."

"Exactly," Dee said. "That's why we must report on what the group out there is all about. Did Larry say if anything can be done to get Cat to back off?"

"Ya, he was on his way to talk with her. I don't know what he'll say, but I'd bet all the change in my pocketbook that he won't let her off easy. Let's hope, anyway."

Will had listened intently to the discussion.

"I don't really have my foot in the door yet," he said, "but if you want, I could go see them. Perhaps a man would have an easier time of it than a woman, do you think?"

Dee thought it over before answering, "No, I think Astrid will be able to do it without difficulty. She has background in dealing with difficult situations, and that will help."

He didn't look disappointed, but quickly said, "I see."

Astrid didn't mention her intention of getting a man to go with her, however. That might make him feel unwanted. Instead, she said, "If I run into trouble, Will, I'll give you a call, and you can come rescue me."

"I guess I might end up calling you for help if I went."

It was good that they could talk easily, Astrid thought. The job seemed to mean a lot to him, no doubt because he was hurting for money, judging from his poor clothing and old shoes again today.

"If I may change the subject," he said, "there's a sign on the way to the motel where I'm staying…"

"The stripper sign?" Dee said.

"Have you done a story on it already? I was under the impression no one had interviewed the man who put it up."

"No. We hadn't gotten to it," Dee said.

"Okay. Well, I didn't have much to do over the weekend so I looked the guy up on Saturday."

"You found out who put up the sign?"

"It turned out to be easy. I stopped in at the Main Street Bakery, and asked the man there if he knew who owned the property and what he planned to do with it."

"Oh yes," Astrid said. "Sonny. I stopped there every morning when I was temporarily living at the motel. I didn't think about it before, but of course he'd know if anyone would."

"He told me it's owned by Bud Small. Apparently he thought the sign would be an attention-getter for his business."

"What is that?" Dee asked.

"He repairs and refinishes furniture."

"You interviewed him?"

"I did. Do you want the story for this week? He won't be able to start building until spring, of course."

"Did he object to a story this soon? Maybe he'd like to wait and let people guess for a while."

"No. He said to go ahead and print the story. He'll take out a big ad when he's ready to start up his business."

"Fine. Then write it. We could use more copy this week. Astrid, will you hang around a bit before going to Greenboro? Charlie should be here soon, but I think he'll take an hour or two this morning to help Jen before coming in. When I was going to have Charlie cover the militia story, I thought he might spend a couple days at the camp, but it's probably wiser not to do it that way after all. We need to exercise caution rather than boldness with the unknown out there."

"Charlie doesn't have children, does he?" Astrid had wanted to ask that for some time.

"Yes," Dee said. "He has two. Beautiful girls, of course, just like their mother. They'll be staying with Jenny's parents until the end of the school year. Maybe then Charlie and Jen will have found a house to buy here. For now, they have just a one-bedroom apartment."

The other question Astrid wanted to ask was one she probably never would ask: did Dee have children? Since Dee never spoke of any, she presumed her marriage had not produced any.

"Now we all have stories to write," Dee said.

As the morning wore on, Astrid became concerned. With each passing half hour she worried that Charlie might not get here today. If it became too late, darkness could overtake her out there at the camp, and that wasn't an exciting thought. Unconsciously, she twisted her ring while she thought of the many accusations Cat Cotter had made about the group, variously calling them KKK and militant misfits, among other disturbing labels.

"Astrid," Dee said at last. "You'll twist your finger off with that ring."

Astrid looked down and realized what she'd been doing.

"If you're caught up for now, go along. Charlie will be here soon. He hasn't called to say otherwise, so I know he'll be here. You have time to get out there, do the interview, and get back before supper."

"Ya. I'll go then. Thanks."

She was ready to go in a few seconds, then thought to call Abram, in case she should be late getting home.

He answered quickly.

"Hi, Dear," she said. "Are you going to work today?'

"They want me for the four to 12 shift today. So I won't be here when you come home."

"Oh. Well, that's okay. It's good that you can get back."

She didn't mention the Greenboro visit, not wanting to get into a possible discussion over it again.

"Anyway," he said, "I'll see you when you get home."

"You bet. Love you."

Astrid said to Dee, "Abram is working tonight at the Sheriff's Office, so when I get back, I'll stay and write my story."

"Okay," Dee said. "But don't stay too late. You'll have a few hours tomorrow morning. Be careful."

Outside the office door, Astrid looked across the hallway toward the advertising and business department, hesitated, shook her head, and walked on down the hall, out to the parking lot, where she got into her Jeep without anyone to go with her.

Dammit, I don't need a baby sitter. What's a man going to do there anyway? Stare them all down? When they see that I'm just a reporter trying to get an accurate story about them, they'll cooperate. I don't need a guard, armed or otherwise.

CHAPTER 16

Once she left the city, she found that the narrower countryside roads had higher banks of snow, sometimes obscuring traffic approaching from a side street. Despite bright sunshine there had been no melting weather for a couple of weeks so some of the roads were still covered with frozen hard-packed snow, making them slick. Driving farther into the country, Astrid thought of Florida and the fact that when they had a cold front go through, they never had to shovel snow nor did drivers have to worry about ending up in the ditch on slippery going. However, she still liked the North Country best and most likely would never retire to a Florida community as so many did.

She had driven some 25 miles to just beyond the border of Greenboro and she started to look for the turnoff to this camp they called The Kingdom. What a joke. Would she find a man dressed in royal robes sitting on a throne? Maybe she'd have to bow to him, call him Your Royal Highness.

Her thoughts were running wild and she understood why. This whole scenario was becoming less and less desirable as she drove along looking for the run-down schoolhouse that would signify the place to turn. She passed two side roads before she saw it, turned left and found herself on a bumpier road. She wove her way around the occasional pot hole for about a mile until she saw what she came for, a hand-painted sign announcing The Kingdom, and beneath that another sign, also tacked to a tree, reading Enter At Your Own Risk and in black paint under that, a ragged swastika.

Nice warm welcome, I must say. Not exactly what I expected.

But it couldn't discourage her. She took the risk, drove on until the road petered out, and unexpectedly found herself on a smooth, black-top road that widened and widened until it turned into a parking area, clear of snow. Parked here were two dump trucks and several Jeeps, as well as a limousine and a number of vehicles, mostly Cadillacs.

What is this? No pick-up trucks. No old Fords. Not a poor man's campground, for sure.

She drove across the lot to the center of a huge compound. It looked too upscale to be a military base. One by one, men in brown uniform pants, sheepskin-lined jackets, and black fur Cossack hats emerged from the brick duplexes. Each man carried a weapon pointed toward the ground. Cat Cotter's words, "They're dangerous," took on new meaning. Indeed, they appeared dangerous and unfriendly. Astrid felt like she had driven into a foreign prison camp, about to be pulled from her Jeep and stood against a wall to face the firing squad.

Stop this right now. They won't hurt you.

But that thought did nothing to alleviate her misgiving over coming here alone. Why didn't she stop at the lab and get a man to come with her? Well, it was too late now. She looked around to see how she might get away even now, just as a tall red-haired man with an equally red mustache stalked out of the huge building on her left. She rolled down her window, but left the engine running.

He stopped a few feet from the Jeep, his long legs wide apart.

With a shotgun held high, he demanded in a mountaineer's voice, "Are you lost?"

"No. I'm…"

"What do you want?"

Give me a chance to tell you.

Her voice met his in volume. "I'm a reporter from Fairchance, and I came here to learn more about your organization."

"Organization? What are you looking for? We're just a group of peace-loving people who enjoy the country air and a bit of target practice."

His mocking tone turned Astrid's fear to anger.

"That's not what I hear. I hear that you have a militia training camp here. Do you care to discuss it with me or not?"

Two men walked closer to the Jeep. The odor from them was one she recognized from her hunting days on the farm…musk used to attract buck deer. She disliked the odor so much she never used it, but men didn't seem to be bothered by it. These men had been hunting, even though the legal hunting season ended over a month ago.

"Can you and I sit down indoors and discuss this? It's cold out here," she said.

"Your name?"

"Astrid Lincoln."

"Leo Metcalf. Get out and go to the first building on the left."

He waved the shotgun in the direction of what appeared to be an armory with flags waving on each side of the marble steps: the U.S. flag and a red one with white circle and black swastika. Maybe they were here just to target practice for fun, but it certainly had all the appearance of a Nazi headquarters, even though the brick duplexes might be found in any middle-class neighborhood.

"And leave my Jeep here? In the middle of the…" she didn't know how to describe this area. Maybe compound or parade ground. They must have a word for this open space. The buildings didn't form a cul-de-sac, since there appeared to be a road extending beyond the houses at the opposite end.

"It's okay right there. Leave it. And leave the keys in it."

Oh no, she wouldn't do that. No one was going to come and drive her Jeep away somewhere. She turned off the ignition and in one motion pulled out the keys. Alighting, she shoved her gloved hand into her heavy jacket pocket and dropped the keys out of sight.

A pathway opened among the armed guards, and she did as the general commanded, walked toward the structure that looked to be about the length of a football field, telling herself to ignore the shotgun at her back and all the other weapons around her.

Before climbing the steps, another thought began to nag. What if she took off her left glove and they saw the precious ring? What would they do then? Take it from her? After all, it was an antique, worth thousands, she was certain. She never knew why Abram seemed displeased with it, though. For whatever reason, she found herself thinking what she'd heard him whisper from time-to-time, "damned ring."

All at once Astrid felt that nagging stomach discomfort that she had when she faced the gun Jimmy held on her in October, threatening to kill her. Only here there were at least two dozen weapons. She attempted a smile, but feared it looked more like a grimace when the chief honcho pulled his shotgun higher, pointed in the direction of her face.

I wish I'd let Abram know where I was going. I wish I hadn't come alone. Hell, I wish I hadn't come at all.

. . . .

Roy had listened to the typewriter all morning, and his anger had risen with the sound of each carriage return bell. Hadn't

Cat done enough damage already? Sheriff Knight cautioned her against writing damning letters when she had no proof to back up her suppositions. He told her she was spreading fear among Fairchance citizens. It wasn't right. If there were more public gatherings among the populace to discuss possible action against those camped out in Greenboro, he would arrest her for inciting a riot.

Why wouldn't that woman understand that these were not the killers who shot her brother? Why did she insist on causing them grief when they hadn't shown any sign of hurting anyone? When he asked her these questions she pouted and said, "The guns. No one has a lot of guns without meaning to do harm to others."

Maybe she was right. Maybe they were learning maneuvers that could be harmful to peaceful citizens, but like the sheriff said, until there was an incident that menaced the welfare of others, his hands were tied. And that's what he wanted Cat's to be--tied.

With that conversation still crystal clear in his mind, Roy left his reading chair and went to the study where Cat worked. She hunched over the typewriter, concentrating on her words so intently that she didn't see or hear him approach. When he spoke, she jumped to her feet in surprise.

"Oh sorry, my dear. I didn't mean to startle you. What are you working on now?"

He tried to sound honestly interested in what she was writing, without being critical at the same time. He'd like to take her by the scruff of the neck and walk her out of the house to cool off. But he would never hurt her, and prided himself that he seldom spoke harshly.

"Did I disturb you, Roy? Well, I'm finished now. Go back to your reading. I won't make any more noise today."

She gathered several of the pages she had typed into an even pile, opened the top drawer to get a large paper clip and clipped them together.

"Don't you want to join me?" he said. "You have a book to finish, don't you?"

"I'll straighten out my desk first. You know I don't like to leave an untidy desk."

"Okay. Come in when you're finished."

He wanted to see what she'd written, but knowing Cat, she'd probably hide it somewhere, so that he couldn't. His only hope was that she hadn't written another letter to the editor.

. . . .

Jenny had to remind Charlie of the time. As with everything else he did, time meant nothing to him when he wanted to finish a task. Now he'd be very late getting to the office.

"You really ought to give it up for today," she said. "Look at the time, Charlie. Those shelves can be done another day. Didn't you tell me the newspaper deadline is tomorrow noon? Here it is almost 11 o'clock. Dee will be coming to drag you over there if you don't get moving."

"I hate to leave this half done."

She looked around at the small, one-bedroom apartment. Thanks to Dee, yesterday they had all the cupboards scrubbed and settled. That was the job she had dreaded most, but here it was all done. The clothes were all hung up in the closets. Charlie had painted the bathroom a peach color, and now he was making shelves for the broom closet, a large space off the entryway. All-in-all, she thought it was a very nice, cozy place for just the two of them over the next two or three months, until they could find something more permanent. They were used to that rambling mansion Dee had inherited and sold to them years ago. Jen was happy to have less housecleaning to do and more time for her art.

Fortunately this apartment had a front bay window where she could set up her work. She wouldn't try to get everything out, only the sketching materials, for now.

"Come on, Honey," she pleaded. "You need to get to the office.

"I'm going. I'm going. Just don't pick up anything. I'll get back to the shelves tonight. And don't bother to make supper. We can go out to eat."

"That's nice," Jenny said. "What about lunch?"

"I'll pick up a sub on the way there."

She waited in the kitchen until he came out in a fresh shirt and clean pants, handed him his winter jacket, and gave him a kiss on the cheek.

"See you later, then," she said. "Love you."

. . . .

Abram went to work early. Still on the learning curve, he wanted to watch while someone else manned the dispatch station for about half an hour. He had done the work before they went to Florida, but that seemed like a year ago now, and he felt like a beginner all over again.

The crisp air hit his lungs like a blow to the chest when he left the car to walk to the Sheriff's Office. Abram wouldn't have it any other way, however. He never liked hot weather and even though Florida was cold when they visited, he could tell that he wouldn't be happy there for very long if it had been the opposite--really hot.

Freddy was alone in the dispatch room. He looked up and said, "Good to see you back, Abram. How you feeling? Put your lunch in the file cabinet over there."

He set the paper lunch bag where he was told, and took a

folding chair from under the bench. He sat near Freddy and leaned forward to better watch.

"I'm almost 100 percent," he said. "Busy today?"

"Naw, not much going on. I guess that's a good sign, huh? I thought we might get a frantic call from that Cat Cotter's husband saying she'd been attacked." He laughed. "You read the letter in yesterday's paper?"

"Yeah. She's a real nut-case, I guess. You really think anyone would attack her? I understand the group she wrote about is camped in woods near Greenboro."

"You never know. We've had stranger things happen. Wait a sec. Here's a call."

It was just a deputy checking in.

When he finished taking the report, Freddy said, "That's the way it's been all day. You'll have a quiet evening, no doubt. You here til midnight?"

"Yup. The bewitching hour."

"Okay. Both the sheriff and Detective Green said they'd be home if they're needed. Of course you don't call the sheriff unless it's a case of murder or something equally serious."

"I remember," Abram said. "Do you have to call them often?"

"Naw, not much. I had to call the sheriff one night when a man in one of those upstairs apartments downtown was drunk and threatening to jump off the top of his building."

"What happened? Did he jump?"

"No. All talk. He just wanted attention is my guess."

"How did they get him down?"

"The sheriff is real good at negotiating with nut cases like that. I guess he just talked him out of the idea and city police put him in the lockup for the rest of the night so he could sober up. One of the deputies said the man cried like a baby. He was upset because his wife left him. I think I'd get drunk, too, to celebrate."

Abram chuckled a bit, but he thought about Astrid. What would he do if she left him? He'd about go crazy, for sure,

A couple more officers checked in, then Freddy asked, "How did the honeymoon go? Did you go anywhere besides the hotel room?"

He winked when he said that.

"The best part of the honeymoon *was* the room. But the rest of it was a cold time. We almost got on a ship for an eastern Caribbean cruise, but we heard that everyone was disappointed when they got back to port. They said it was too cold and windy to get off the ship at ports of call. So we just caught the next bus back to the motel. And then a funny thing happened. The new editor called Astrid and said they needed her at the office. It didn't take us long to pack and get onto a plane headed north."

"You park your car at the airport, did you?"

"Yeah, and it was buried. But neither one of us cared. We were just glad to be home."

Freddy chuckled. "I can see you're born jet setters."

"How about you? Ever been on a cruise?"

"Naw. I've never been anywhere except right here in the good ol' State of Maine. It's good enough for me."

Freddy was ready to leave.

"It's quiet now. You should be okay," he said."

"I will."

"It's all yours, then. You want me to stick around for a few minutes?"

"No. Go on home. If I have a question, I'll give you a call."

After Freddy left, Abram had a fleeting moment of panic on the first call, but soon calmed down. He even let himself think of Astrid until the next call, wondering if she'd miss him this evening. But, of course, she had been alone enough years that she wouldn't give him a second thought. He hoped she hadn't gone out to Greenboro, but at least she wouldn't go alone. He could call the office and find out, but it wouldn't be right to interrupt her work. This was a busy day for the newspaper editors.

She'll be okay. My girl is no weakling, as sweet as she is. I just wish I hadn't agreed to take that ring from Gunnar. For that matter, I should have told her about it already. That damned ring. Sometimes I think it really is cursed. Seems like all we've had is trouble since I put it on Astrid's finger.

CHAPTER 17

Astrid kept her left glove on, as well as her other outer garments, though the room where Leo Metcalf took her felt quite warm after being in the freezing air outside. The opulence of this huge apartment opened Astrid's eyes to one aspect of the training camp, even in a cursory study: these people did not live poorly.

Red leather chairs and sofa set an elegant tone for the living room, complemented by a Persian rug. Large, colorful paintings warmed winter white walls. Several weapons were displayed in an oversize glass case, and a curved leather-top desk at the end of the room looked like pictures she'd seen of the president's Oval Office desk. At the opposite end of the room, a long bar fronted a kitchenette. The bar stools were also red leather. Shelves of liquor bottles lined the side wall beyond the bar.

Astrid glimpsed doors along the hallway beyond the kitchenette, presumably to bedrooms and bathrooms.

"You live here year-round?" she asked.

"Some of us do, and others don't. I'm here year-round. This is headquarters."

"And families?"

"Certainly. We have a small school, a basic medical clinic, a store."

"I noticed the gas pumps out in the parking lot."

"The Kingdom will one day be on the map as an incorporated town. We're almost there now, but a few more details need to be worked out."

"Quite impressive, I must say. This building is huge."

"We have important visitors on occasion," he said, "who require overnight quarters, so behind the stage in the auditorium is a guest suite, smaller than this one. We also have a conference room on the other side."

"It's very nice," She brought out her tape recorder and questioned with a gesture whether he was okay with it, to which he nodded.

"This past summer we completed the last few buildings that you saw for the men and their wives and others who come for training. We seldom fill the auditorium to capacity when we have a weekend retreat for those interested in joining maneuvers, but it can accommodate 500 people."

"That many? Out here?"

"We're attracting the attention of people not just in Maine, but also New Hampshire and Massachussetts. Doesn't matter where something is held, if people are interested enough, they will find it."

"Not the greatest road to come in on, however."

"That will be upgraded next summer."

"If I may get personal, are you married?"

"Mmm. My wife comes here some, but she enjoys city life, lots of social activity. She's in Florida right now."

"And children?"

"Two. My son Leon teaches history in Alabama. My daughter Destiny trains horses in Kentucky."

"That's interesting. Destiny is an unusual name, too."

"My wife's name is Darlene and she wanted our daughter

to have the same initials that she has, just as Leon has mine. Somehow she thought Destiny signified importance. And my daughter is that--important." He looked down at a family photo on the coffee table. "In my eyes, at least."

Something wrong with her? Astrid wondered.

"You're from the South."

"Sure am. Alabama." He laughed. "You don't miss much do you?"

"It would be hard to miss that vernacular."

"Most of our men are married, and their wives train right along with them. Some have children here, too, not below ten years old. And there are a few singles who pair up with a friend. My daughter comes for a couple of weeks each summer and brings a friend."

Though he seemed friendly enough, he still had the shotgun, resting across the chair arms, not pointed directly at her, but he could put a shot close enough for a few pellets to hit her in a vital spot. The threat was too obvious, and she couldn't relax. She judged him to be vain, rich, and untrustworthy. That word, the one Cat was fond of using, kept coming to mind...dangerous.

"Mr. Metcalf..."

"*General* Metcalf," he corrected. "See these four stars? They stand for general. I'm a general, Miss Lincoln."

"It's *Mrs.* Lincoln, General." She refrained from showing him her ring. "I'm married. You have U.S. Army ranks, then?"

"That's right. We're militia. This one is only the beginning of a movement that will come to life everywhere. They've begun to grow in a few other states. Believe me, when militia training takes off, all 16 counties in Maine will have a camp, not up to the standards here, but training camps of some sort. This will be the high command post, and of course, I will be commander over all the operations. Our outreach will be even greater than this state, with ranks from private to lieutenant general under my command."

"To what end?"

"The Patriot movement, which needs more positive publicity, will provide what the country needs--renewal. Training here will ensure that we are ready to protect Americans. Mark my words, this is only the beginning of a movement that will free this country from tyranny."

The general assumed a far-away look, as if he might be seeing the vast empire he would command. He leaned over the shotgun, holding it steady with both hands.

"Did you notice any overhead lines when you came in? No, you didn't, because we have them all underground. A complex communication system was the first thing we installed. I'll show you the communications center on our way out, but you can't take pictures there. We have a couple of areas that must not be photographed. I'll tell you as we come to them. And I want no pictures taken of me. Understand?"

She nodded, though she had planned to take only his photo and not to go roaming about the grounds.

"Of course, if that's what you want."

"This compound was carefully planned. When it's finished it will be the most modern camp of all the United Patriots."

"United Patriots?"

She'd heard that name before. Cat Cotter wrote the name in something she sent out for newspapers.

"That's right. It will be a unified force. When I bring all of the camps under one umbrella, it will be called Infinite Patriots, leaders forever. We will be prepared to fight oppressive power. We'll save this country and the world."

He pounded his fist on the table. "It's time citizens recognize governmental illegalities and corruption, like the IRS, for instance."

"It sounds like an impossibly ambitious goal."

"Nothing's impossible. It just takes planning and training."

"So you are antigovernment."

"What will come, will come. We're preparing for worst scenarios. We'll meet the challenge of any threat to life and liberty."

"Can you be more specific? How will you do that?"

"It will likely begin when the government starts to take away our guns. They will, you know. They'll try to strip us of all our rights and protections, especially our weapons. But, without revealing just how, I'll tell you that we're already prepared to counteract that."

Astrid didn't question that statement. No doubt plenty of weapons were hidden in these woods.

"You really think the government would go after your guns?"

She thought of Cat Cotter and how that would please her.

"Don't be naïve. They'll do it. Little by little they'll chip away at our gun ownership rights. But we'll be ready. Let me tell you, we're the true Patriots, not those pinheads in Washington who are controlled by bankers, Wall Street, lobbyists. Every one of our so-called representatives in Washington can be bought, and most of them have been. The country is run by the super rich and infidels who worship the almighty dollar."

"But you aren't a poor group here, obviously."

"We're ordinary citizens. Those who come here pay their dues and help with running the place. We have no slackers here."

"And all this is for protection," she said. "You think there's a real need for armed protection."

"There will be. And we will be ready. We will fight until we return the country to what the founding fathers envisioned when they drew up the Constitution."

"That's an extreme statement," she said. "It sounds like you plan more than a passive existence here in the woods to get ready for something that may or may not come along. It sounds like preparation for aggressive terrorism."

His face and body stiffened in agitation.

"We're not criminals and we're not anarchists. We're not planning to overthrow the government. But we will protect our Christian country against tyranny, corruption in government, unconstitutional legislation and taxation. Without training like ours, who will save this nation? We must take charge before the country is run by so many factions that it will no longer be the same nation, the nation that worships God. This country should not allow interracial marriages and an influx of the wrong people."

She understood what he meant, but decided to make him say it.

"Do I detect racial prejudice in your objectives?"

"The races should be pure. Our ancestors were white Anglo-Saxon. We must strive to keep that purity of race. White men wrote the Constitution. They didn't go out and recruit a few blacks to help them define our Republic."

"No. But the Civil War was fought and the 13th Amendment was enacted to abolish slavery. If I recall correctly, the country was supposed to welcome all types. I don't remember any restrictions on race or ethnicity."

General Metcalf glared, staring her down as if she had just slapped him in the face.

"Don't give me that crap, young lady. History teaches that slavery was not invented by the United States. There have always been superior minds over inferior ones who did the work. They're the drones, the slaves, if you like. The dominant always rule, naturally. We should breed for strength and intelligence."

Before he became too disturbed, Astrid attempted another approach.

"You put a lot of energy into physical fighting. Why not turn that energy into work that would change the system, the way it's set up, by campaigning for honest men and women in Congress, making sure that our laws don't infringe on the rights of voters?"

"Loyalties in our government are not only bought, but in turn, officials themselves buy loyalties. The problem with common society today is that people in general expect to be taken care of. They accept government supports, entitlements. Entitlements? They're no more entitled than I am, and I don't call on for everything. I worked to get where I am. I pay for my medical bills, my food. But, mark my words, these entitlements are no more than scraps from very rich plates."

She avoided the obvious, which she had researched before coming here. General Metcalf had served in the U.S. Army.

"You don't believe in helping the poor get on their feet?"

"I'm a generous man. But I won't support those who won't get off their rear ends and help themselves. It's that simple."

"I doubt it's that simple."

He appeared ready to give her an argument, but closed his mouth. While she waited for him to collect his thoughts, she looked around at all the decorations, consisting mostly of war memorabilia—swords, old guns, war books. On the coffee table was a single book, *The Turner Diaries*, and she wondered what that was. Before she could ask, he began again.

"The American public isn't prepared for the collapse of government. People don't foresee disaster. They can't imagine a time when all of civilization falls to its knees and begs for support. But then, of course, it will be too late. No one will remain to fight the forces of evil, because people will have become soft and selfish. They'll riot and steal and destroy. They've been mired in the mud of greed so long that they aren't prepared to take care of themselves. You see? The only ones who will be prepared are the private armies, the militias. We're the ones who will fight for a peaceful world. We'll go back to basics and bring back the Constitution."

Astrid had to think about that. He talked as if he were on a platform calling the country to war. He sounded pedantic, like he had been duly elected to the presidency and had a mandate to dictate to the masses.

"You have me confused. Are you building up your militia for a fight now or for something you expect to happen several years from now?"

"Any time, now or later." He waved his hand wide demonstrating the width of time and space for fighting. "If we must attack certain known capitalistic fortresses in order to stop an anti-Christ takeover of the country, then we will do it sooner, rather than later."

"Anti-Christ? So, you're not anarchists, and yet you're obviously against the government, our democratic policies, and apparently against some established religions. It sounds to me as if you're against all that this country stands for…freedom of religion, the right to vote, equal representation in Congress. Not only that, but what you just said sounds very much like you plan an assault on anything that contradicts what *you* believe in. I'm having trouble sorting out just what you do believe in. Anti-Christ is a controversial term that could suggest opposition to just about any theology. Then you are fundamentalists?"

"I just say that the devil himself leads the lawmakers, flashing thousand dollar bills in their faces. As the Bible states, they worship filthy lucre."

"I'd say you and your group are all as wealthy as those you're against."

His hands gripped the shotgun harder.

"We earned our money, it wasn't handed to us for favors. Every man and woman here is Christian. We know what's right and wrong. We have to resist the temptation to lie back and wait. We refuse to be bought or to be treated like dogs at the table, waiting for scraps to fall our way. I repeat, we'll protect the values of this country."

Astrid began to feel uncomfortable hearing radical views and goals that smacked of Nazism. Perhaps they were terrorists, though he spoke of their Christianity as if they were saintly. His wild talk was filled with anger, directed at the government.

"I just can't understand what you expect you will do, when, or why actually."

"Let me put it this way. Come the revolution—words you've heard before, no doubt—we'll be leading the way."

This was more than she could handle all in one sitting. Her own thoughts were beginning to jumble. She had never before engaged in such a radical discussion and decided she had enough. She needed to wind up the interview and get back to Fairchance, to return to sanity. But she had one more topic that they hadn't discussed.

"Did you read yesterday's Bangor newspaper?"

"Yes, I read it."

He took the paper from the middle shelf in his chair stand.

"And did you read the letter to the editor by Cat Cotter?"

"It's right here. She's a stupid woman who has no idea what she's talking about. Do you work with her?"

"No. I'm the news editor for *The Bugle* in Fairchance. I'm here to get your response to the letter. As far as I can tell, you are just what she claims you are, a militia group bent on working outside the law. Do Fairchance residents need to worry that you and your men will come into town and start shooting?"

"We're militia, as in the Second Amendment. You know. The

one that says, 'A well regulated militia, being necessary to the security of a free State, the right of the people to keep and bear arms shall not be infringed.' We carry arms. My men can use them effectively. And we have that right."

"I don't know many who can recite an amendment word for word," Astrid said. "I do know that states' well-regulated militias were formed, and the Constitution was written, in the days when they had to protect themselves from Indian attacks, as well as attacks by sea. Maine's militia became the National Guard, and still exists to aid in times of crises. Why not just join up with them?"

He looked and sounded angry.

"We're more than that. We're protecting from attacks within as well as outside our country."

"There are no more Indian attacks. You're aiming at the government. Or do you expect an invasion?"

"You never know. Invasion. Political repression. Proclamation to relinquish arms. There's any number of reasons why it's necessary to be prepared."

"I saw the swastika at the entrance and the one on your flag. Are you neo-Nazis? White supremacists?"

Again, he was red-faced.

"In its original, true meaning, the swastika was a symbol of good fortune, of life and joy. For us, it symbolizes hope for the future when the country will return to true freedom. We'll not stand by and watch our rights eroded one by one. Isn't this being a good citizen, to act as a watchdog for society?"

"Some say the watchdog can be too aggressive, that instead of protecting the rights of the public, it attacks individuals' right to privacy, as well as all that the Constitution stands for, including the duly elected government representatives."

General Metcalf let out a belly laugh that surprised Astrid. What was his game? Was he deliberately baiting her, making fun of her for pointing out the fears that people like Cat Cotter expressed?

"That's a damned big laugh from a man who leads a bunch of thugs," she said.

Immediately, she knew she had gone too far when his laugh turned into a snarl and his green eyes narrowed. But she was in it now.

"Thugs! You're treading on thin ice, *Mrs.* Lincoln. What an appropriate name. Are you here for a non-biased story or do you plan to put out a call to arms against us? Perhaps to free my slaves of free-thinking? You should find out just how well prepared we are to protect ourselves. I think we'll have to demonstrate our maneuvers for you. The men are about to begin target and bayonet practice. I'll take you to the range for observation. This is all perfectly legal. We are, you see, within our lawful rights."

"But you pick and choose the laws to follow."

"Perhaps so. Doesn't everyone pick and choose what rules they will follow? Even church members select the tenets that they accept. As the old woman said during Sunday service, 'Now he's stopped preaching and started meddling.' Yes, I see that you find that amusing. Sin is okay when it's your own sin of choice. Am I wrong?"

"But you're saying everyone must live under *your* version of right. Am *I* wrong?"

"By God, you enjoy a fight, I see. I like that. You should join us. Seriously. You'd make a good soldier. You look strong. You're as tall as most of my men. You have a commanding voice. You'd advance in rank in no time. Come out on a weekend and join the fun."

"It's not my thing, thank you."

She'd been studying the guns in the case behind him, able to identify a few, but not all.

"Do I see assault weapons in that case?"

"Absolutely. We have every kind of weapon you can name. But, I don't need to tell you. If you join us, you'll learn all about these weapons, how to disassemble and reassemble them in seconds. Ever shot a gun?"

"Yes. On the farm we all went hunting to put meat on the table. Not to shoot people."

"You make shooting people sound like it's unthinkable. I tell you right now if outside terrorists or our own government agents start marching citizens off to prison, or come through your town raping and killing, you'll gladly pick up a weapon and shoot people. This Cotter woman wrote a slanderous piece. She should watch her step. Not everyone tolerates slander. See here?" He held up the paper and pointed to a line. "She says we're a hate group. Where'd she get that? She never came out here and looked into our activity. We don't hate. We face reality."

He stood up.

"Now, Mrs. Lincoln, come with me. We'll see a little action in the field."

"No, General Metcalf. I don't think I'll be staying, despite your gracious invitation. And I know you would not infringe on my rights as a U.S. citizen by holding me a virtual prisoner, would you?"

Astrid was ready to leave. She was sick of this interview and intended to get out of here. She turned off the tape recorder, returned it to her bag, put on her right glove, and started to get out of the chair, when she looked across the room...into the business end of the shotgun.

Damn. Now what do I do?

CHAPTER 18

Darkness had settled half an hour ago, and Dee was in a full state of worry. Astrid should have been back by now. She said she would return before dark to avoid the possibility of getting lost on the dark country roads around Greenboro.

For the fourth time, Dee picked up the phone to call Astrid's house. And for the fourth time, there was no answer. She hesitated about calling the Sheriff's Office for fear of alarming Abram, but it seemed just too dangerous not to.

Everything had been going smoothly all day, especially after both Charlie and Will came in. Will's experience became apparent when he wrote the story on Strippers in a half hour. Charlie then told him to check out a police call they heard over the scanner, indicating an attack on a girl at the college, and he soon had the facts. A college youth had brought a bottle of gin back to school following a weekend at home and decided to have a party in his room. It became unruly and he left the others, who were still drinking, while he took a walk outside.

The young woman, also a student at Fairchance College, met him on a walk way, he lost his balance when he tried to avoid bumping into her, and fell against her. From there, it became touch and go, as the investigating policeman said with tongue in cheek, she called the police, and the youth was taken away to sober up in a jail cell. No charges were made, but Will quoted the young woman as saying, "He's a drunken brute."

Now Will had gone home, Charlie was stacking the several piles of papers on his desk, and Dee looked about for something to do besides think of Astrid.

"You're worried," Charlie said.

Dee wanted to say that she was ready to scream with anxiety. Instead, she pushed the telephone away, and settled back in her chair. If she showed too much concern, Charlie would remain with her, and he needed to get back to Jenny. He had said that he was going to take her out to supper.

"I'm sure she's all right," Dee said. "You don't need to stay. Jen is waiting for you. I'll wait a bit longer and make a couple more calls."

"You sure about that? I don't mind staying with you, if you think it might help."

"What can you do? What can anyone do? It's one of those times when we just have to wait and see."

He changed from his shoes to warm boots, and put the shoes under his desk, got his coat and hesitated at the door.

"Okay then," he said. "I'll call in after we have supper. But you won't wait here that long, will you?"

"I...don't really know. Depends on whether I find out anything. No, just go. If she comes in, I'll call you. Where are you taking Jenny?"

"Well, I got kind of used to the meals at the Edge of Town Restaurant. I think we'll go there."

"It's a great place to eat. Enjoy. I can call you there."

After he was gone, Dee pulled the phone toward her and sat with hand poised to dial, debating the call to Larry Knight. She lifted the receiver and started to punch in the numbers when the door opened.

135

"Marvin," she said, and put the receiver back in its cradle. "Come in. What brings you over here?"

"I was going to my car when I noticed your lights still on. Anything wrong?"

"How I wish I knew the answer to that. Astrid went out to Greenboro to talk with the people at that camp, The Kingdom. She should have been back two hours ago, and I'm very worried that something has happened."

"Can you call them out there?"

"They don't have a listed number. I was just about to call Sheriff Knight. The only problem with that is Abram. I don't want to alarm him just yet."

"Why would he be alarmed?"

"He works for the sheriff now as a dispatcher and Astrid said he's working this evening."

"I see. Well, you might call State Police in the Greenboro area. They can go to the camp and see if she has left. If she did leave an hour or so ago, then the police can go along the route she took and search."

"Oh lord. I hope she hasn't had an accident."

"Call the police and start the ball rolling. Chances are she was delayed and simply didn't get away as soon as she thought she would."

"You're right. I'll do that," Dee said. "Wait a minute. State Police will put out an APB and local authorities will get it. Abram will hear it. I can't do that."

"Did she go alone?"

"She had said she'd get someone to go with her, but as far as I can determine, she didn't. I've never put anyone in danger like this before. I knew Charlie should have gone, although I don't know if he could have done better than she can."

"I read the letter that Mrs. Cotter wrote. I hope they aren't as bad as she paints them."

Dee choked up when she thought of the trouble Astrid could be in.

"I hope not. I hope not."

She dropped her head to her hands.

"And the roads are dark and probably slippery out in the country. Oh…" She could say no more, but felt Marvin's arm around her shoulders, pulling her to him.

"Trust that she's okay, my dear. She's strong, and most likely can handle about anything thrown at her."

At that, Dee giggled, reacting to nerves more than humor.

"I hope they aren't throwing things at her."

She leaned her head on Marvin's arm. The nearness of another human being had a calming effect. They remained that way, Dee sitting at her desk with her head on Marvin's arm, and he stroking her hair, until she looked into his eyes. His sudden kiss surprised but didn't disturb her in the least. They said nothing.

The silence was broken when the door opened again, and this time it was Astrid.

"Thank God," Dee said.

Nearly toppling Marvin, she rushed to Astrid and threw her arms about her waist.

"Are you okay? I was worried when it got dark. What happened? Why are you so late?"

"It's a long story, but I'll tell you this. I was never so glad to get away from a place as I was that one. You just wouldn't believe what it is. We thought it would be a rough band of men out target practicing and pretending to be soldiers. Well, it's a whole lot more than that."

. . . .

Cat glared at her husband. She looked around the desk to find something to throw at him.

"Cat, don't do something foolish. You know I'm right. Any more of these letters could bring a lawsuit, if nothing else. You've got our neighbors so upset with your constant wild talk that they don't speak to me any more when I'm outside. Do you really want to be a pariah? Don't you want to live in peace with your neighbors and friends like we always did? When did you plan a bridge party last? Or even go to see Patsy? And she's our next-door neighbor, for heaven's sake. I'm not going to stand for this any longer. If you don't stop all the crazy talk and the letter-writing, I'll see to it that you go away for a few months of treatment. Is that what you want?"

Cat's brain felt like it would burst out of her skull. What could she do? She couldn't hurt Roy, but she was furious with him over tearing up her last letters to the editor. She would have sent them to the Augusta area newspapers. She even had all the envelopes ready.

"You shouldn't have torn up my letters, Roy. I put a lot of time into them. I should have the right to speak out. After all, this is a free country. Let the neighbors hate me. Better that than being slaughtered in their beds. You watch and see, Roy. It will happen. And then you'll be sorry that you and everyone else wouldn't pay attention and do something to stop them."

"Cat, my dear. Please listen to me. Authorities will take care of any threat to our safety. You can trust them to do their job."

Didn't anyone care? Couldn't they see what was happening in this country? People shooting innocent people for no reason. It had to stop. What could she do beyond write letters? There must be a way. She'd get even with Roy. She'd show everyone.

Just wait and see. You'll pay. All you naysayers will pay for calling me mad when I'm the only one who knows just what those animals are capable of.

CHAPTER 19

Astrid didn't know what to think, what to say. Should she just go home and sleep for the night? Maybe her thoughts would come together better in the morning. Looking from Dee to Marvin, she realized that they had worried about her, and now they wanted to know what happened. It wouldn't be right to let them down, no matter how tired and confused she felt.

She went to Charlie's desk and dropped into the chair to face Marvin and Dee. At first she closed her eyes, hardly knowing where to start. Nor did she know if she had the energy to relate the difficulty that she encountered. Dee and Marvin both sat down and waited. She took a deep breath, determined to let it all out.

"The first thing, after you bump over the worst country road ever, you see a black swastika painted on a board outside the gate. There's no guard at the gate, so I was able to drive in. It's a regular little city of duplexes, with a huge auditorium that can hold 500 people, I was told. In the building are a couple of apartments and a conference room, as well.

"General Metcalf runs the place, and he insists on being called general. He says one day all Maine counties will have militia camps, and he'll be the commanding officer over it all. He's self-important. I would go so far as to say he's delusional. He

139

claims he will command all 16 county militias in the future and perhaps others in other states. His talk is confusing. He'll say one thing, maybe contradict it, or he'll sidestep a question entirely. I honestly thought he acted like a dictator, planning to undermine our own government, even to launch war on whatever he thinks is anti-American or a threat to his constitutional rights, or to fundamentalist Christian religions. And that's just about everything."

She was talking too fast, but it was hard to calm down when she had been terrified. For a moment she thought she wouldn't be able to go on. Her lower lip trembled, and she sucked it in to keep from embarrassing herself. She could still see the guns pointed at her and hear the threatening tone of General Metcalf's bellow, "Fire!"

"You know, Cat Cotter was right. I'm convinced that General Metcalf and his troops could very well blow up a school, or a bank, or anything else that he decided would make a clear statement about their power."

"My goodness," Dee said. "Are you sure?"

"Considering his attitude and how he hates the government and financial institutions, yes, I'm quite sure. But he's not the only one there. Every man I talked with echoed his sentiments. Some were even more radical than he was. One man said non-whites and Jews should all be executed. He was the most outspoken one there. He insists the only solution to the country's problems is 'resistance to tyranny by force of arms.' That's an exact quote. He said elections can't fix what ails the country, but a bloody revolution can."

"That's shocking language," Marvin said. "Seditious. Authorities should go out there and shut that place down."

"Apparently there's nothing that can be done. And to tell the truth, maybe arrests are what they want anyway. It would give them an excuse to go after law enforcement. Then they could claim they were being repressed by those who would deny the Patriots their Constitutional rights."

"This is a tough one," Dee said. "Any idea how you'll write it?"

"God only knows," Astrid said. "I think I'll need to talk with authorities before I can safely write about them. If I'm not careful, I could just spark some terrible explosion from them, an attack on innocent people around here."

Marvin was on his feet, pacing, thinking.

"Do you want my suggestion, Dee?"

"Anything. Of course."

"I suggest a short item, with a couple of photos, that gives no hint of the group's ideology, but tells how the men and women go there for the exercises, maybe a direct quote or two from the general--something that doesn't sound too threatening, and quote the sheriff concerning the law as it applies to that type of activity. I'm sure Sheriff Knight will have something to say about it. In other words, soften it. Then go on with an investigation, ranging into federal laws, any problems in other states with this kind of activity. I've never paid much attention, but I seem to recall a couple of incidents that might be worth checking out."

Dee looked at Astrid.

"What do you think?"

"I think that's a good idea. No need to sound an alarm yet."

"No," Dee said. "Maybe they'll just fade away after a while, and we really won't have a thing to worry about after all."

Astrid no longer thought that way. She had gone to Greenboro and visited what she thought would be a harmless group in the woods, only to find that they had no intention of remaining harmless.

"I guess the reason I feel they are dangerous is that they not only have food, medical supplies, weapons and ammunition to

141

last maybe six months, but they are vindictive, the whole kit and kaboodle. I wanted to leave about an hour and a half before I finally could. And the reason I had to stay was that I was held at gunpoint."

"Oh no," Dee said. "Gunpoint. Who did that and why?"

"First the general, holding a shotgun, forced me to the firing range where I watched shooting practice as well as bayonet games. When I finally said I was going to leave, the general ordered his men to point their rifles at me. Then he yelled 'Fire!' and I nearly collapsed. But they all started to laugh. It was a big joke. Lucky for me, I don't have a bad heart."

"That's sick," Marvin said. "You could sue them for endangerment."

"I think, Mr. Cornell, that the old adage 'the word is mightier than the sword' will do the trick. You're right. We need to do a lot of digging. But I know one thing. They need to be stopped. They will do something drastic, something that will cost lives. I don't doubt what terrible acts they're capable of. And the worst of it is that these are not poor, angry people who just want a chance at living a better life. These are wealthy men and women who should be content to have what they have in their upscale homes, working at their well-paid professions. But instead they want to crumble the foundation of what they have…liberty. Listen to me. I sound like the general spouting off. I guess I spent too much time with him. More than I wanted to, for sure."

Astrid saw all that she had experienced with General Metcalf in a seamless re-run, and shook her head.

"I don't think I can write tonight, after all."

"Let me take you two to dinner, then," Marvin said. "How about the Edge of Town Restaurant? It's the closest and the best, besides."

"That's a very good idea," Dee said. "How about it, Astrid? Let's relax over a good meal. You'll feel better. We'll all feel better."

"I think I'll pass tonight, thanks. I just want to go home and lie down for a while before Abram finishes his shift."

"Can't blame you there," Marvin said. "We'll catch you another time. Shall we go, Dee?"

. . . .

At home, sitting on her sofa, Astrid began to shake. Ugly questions haunted her all the way from the office, questions that played over and over in her head. What if they had shot her? Or what if they had taken her Jeep away somehow and made her stay as a "guest"? What if those men had actually fired at her? What if she had gotten lost on that desolate road after dark, or had an accident? What if…what if…what if?

"This has to stop," she said aloud. "I can't think about what didn't happen."

She knew the reason that she had become frightened, and it had to do with her near-death experience in October, when she thought she would die in that awful warehouse. When the handgun went off, she could have been the one shot instead of Jimmy. Since then, she'd noticed her own timidity growing instead of diminishing as it should.

But here she was, in her own home, sitting on her own sofa. She was alive and well, hadn't been in an accident. Abram would be home in a few hours, and they would cuddle for the night, safe and sound, in their own bed.

"So stop this moping, dammit."

She went to the study, found pen and paper, and began to write notes for her story, the one that would tell of a group of men and women at shooting practice in a place called The Kingdom near Greenboro.

. . . .

The next afternoon, Tuesday, Astrid went home to have a snack with Abram, having left him asleep early. She wanted him to read the newspaper story, not to boast, but to relieve his mind. He knew nothing about her encounter with the militia group, and since she had written only a hint of their radicalism, she believed and hoped he would get the impression that all went well and that she had faced no difficulties.

She watched him closely while he read, but could see nothing in his expression to reveal a positive or negative reaction--not until he finished. Then he laid the paper on the table. His head tipped and his eyes narrowed. He knew something.

"Good work, dear," he said. "Now, care to tell me the rest of it?"

"What do you mean?"

She hoped her innocent look would work.

"I mean what about being held at gunpoint?"

"How did you hear about that?"

"You weren't going to tell me, were you? I heard about it from the sheriff's secretary when she called with next week's work schedule. She said, 'That was some fright your wife had with the militia group.' You see, she thought you would have told me. When I insisted she go on, she said you had gone in to talk with Larry and she heard your conversation, being in the next room with the door open and all. So, you want to tell me?"

"I don't want to, no. I don't want to upset you."

"It's too late for that. So you might as well give me the full version."

After she related how she was treated by the men, Astrid got up from the table and went to the counter to refill their coffee cups.

"Let me ask you something," Abram said. "Who did you take with you?"

Damn! Now he'll blow his stack for sure.

She set the cups down on the table and returned to her chair. How could she put this so he wouldn't get angry?

"I couldn't find anyone, and in the interest of time, I left the office alone."

"In other words, you faced…what, 25 or so?…men, all armed, with nothing more for protection than your good looks and a tape recorder?"

"That's about the size of it."

She could see he was struggling with conflicting emotions. On the one hand, he'd like to kill her for her carelessness when she knew it could get rough out there, but on the other hand, he was grateful that she came back to him alive and unharmed.

"That was a dumb thing to do, and you know it," he said. "You're too smart to be getting yourself into these situations. Please promise me you'll think twice before jumping into another dangerous place like that. Promise that you won't tackle an army of men without backup again."

"I don't know what the hell good another body out there would have done. You think a man would have challenged those soldiers? You think they'd have been scared off by a sharp word or a punch in the nose by a man?"

"I think the general would have been less apt to set you up if you'd had a witness to the fake execution. As it is, your word against his and all the others in that crazy troop is useless in the legal world. So, again, will you please not be so bold another time?"

He reached across the table and took her hand in his.

"Please?"

He rolled his fingertip over the wedding ring, and she could almost hear his thoughts: *Damned ring.*

"Ya, I promise, if you promise to explain to me what that means."

"What?"

"When you say 'damned ring.' What is the problem? Are you sorry you married me?"

"Oh, God, no. Never. You're the best thing that ever happened to me. I love you."

"Well then? Will you explain why you say that?"

"I didn't think you ever noticed. I guess I didn't realize I said the words loud enough."

"Ya. You do. And maybe you didn't know that I have very good hearing."

"I know now. I guess I'll have to confess, but you're not going to like it. It's getting late right now. We'll discuss it later. I promise."

CHAPTER 20

Wednesday morning, General Metcalf stood in his living room facing three of his most trustworthy and longest-serving men to prepare them for a secret mission. Until now, he had shared the plot with no one. He could probably accomplish his goal all by himself, but these days it was easier to let the younger men do the grunt work of a mission. If he had his way, he'd take his Ruger Mini-14 semi and lay a few bank executives to rest. Thirty rounds would do the trick easy. He'd wake up Washington. The era of the Infinite Patriots would be launched. In days to come, he himself would lead his militia against inevitable street riots. It would happen. People would panic. It was only a matter of time. He was the leader, the general.

For now, this plan, quite minor in reality, must be formulated, the work must begin. He said, "Men, it's time to meet," and the men took the three seats facing him at his desk. All were silent as he began.

"What is said here this morning is not to be discussed with anyone beyond this room. Not even your wives. Is that understood?"

He looked from one to another.

"Lieutenant Frye, Sergeant Godfrey, Sergeant Norman."

"Yes Sir," they said simultaneously.

"You all read the Fairchance newspaper this week, so you know what our blond visitor wrote. After our conversation two days ago, I'm convinced that this won't be the end of it. She had a broader agenda in coming here, more than just this brief piece. All through our interview, she was trying to trip me up, but I am not easily fooled. I believe that our long-legged lady will pick up on other points, those that she left out of this story. She'll use them and twist the facts into whatever myth she wants to make of our existence. It's only a matter of time now before other newspapers, maybe television, will be knocking at our doors. The media are out to hurt us, and we mustn't let that happen. We're within our God-given rights."

As if choreographed, the men said in one voice, "Yes Sir."

He picked up the newspaper and read: "The Kingdom is no tent city. It consists of brick duplexes and a large headquarters building where General Metcalf resides and where some 500 people can gather to hear talks about the alleged coming militia movement in the state and beyond. This observer noted stores of weapons, food, and ammunition. Altogether, the evidence points to wealthy men and women who congregate for training. Some are permanent residents and some attend on weekends."

General Metcalf stopped reading and removed his glasses to look directly into the eyes of each man.

"You see, she said nothing about our preparations to counteract government's increasing intrusion into citizens' lives, our readiness for the breakdown of society, our opposition to the unlawful tax laws and to unlawful confiscation of weapons. I explained to her how we were here to protect society. But instead of emphasizing any of that, she wrote only about our weaponry and food stockpiles even suggesting we're rich. We need to curb this bad publicity."

He looked from one to another for approval, and each man nodded.

"How will we do that, Sir?" Sergeant Norman asked.

"We want to send all of them a message, Sergeant, but we don't want to leave any evidence that we're the ones who committed the deed. We only want them to expect worse if they don't stop the harassment. Suspicion amounts to message."

He turned his chair sideways and cupped his hands to think. The three men waited quietly.

Turning back, he said, "There are several possible ways to send that message, but we don't want to bring the law to our door. At the same time, media types should understand. I want to scare the shit out of all reporters. It should be something that comes close to Astrid Lincoln."

"Why not just neutralize her, Sir?" Godfrey said.

Godfrey was the coldest of his men, and undoubtedly would kill Astrid with one clean shot and never be identified because no one would see him. But General Metcalf didn't want that to happen. If anything, he'd like to kidnap Astrid, indoctrinate her to the cause, maybe keep her as a close companion. His men didn't need to know that.

"No. We need the press. If we kill the newspaper or do away with the reporters, then we hurt ourselves. If, on the other hand, they get the message, they'll be more charitable, give us some honest reporting. They'll have to. We may even cooperate with them by taking out a few large ads inviting new members."

Frye spoke up, "Sir, we could see that her husband has an unfortunate accident."

"That's a good possibility, Lieutenant, I thought of that. I also thought that the woman who has a poison pen—that Cotter woman-- could be a target. She's a thorn in the side. One shot would drop her. Tragedy comes in all forms.The Swedish lady could become a widow quite tragically with a bit of planning."

"Does she have a pet?" Norman said. "Loss of a pet can be devastating."

"Ah, a pet. We don't have that intelligence yet," General Metcalf said. "It's something that you can find out. But that action could bring retaliation. No. I think not to that idea. You must do surveillance for about a week. Learn the habits of the women and their husbands. From that knowledge, we'll know how to proceed with discretion. You three can work together on the surveillance. Once we find out all we need to know, we'll proceed with a concrete plan. We'll meet back here at the same time a week from today. I'll expect a report from each of you as well as any recommendations you may have on how to proceed."

"You want us to stay in Fairchance at the motel for the week, then?" Godfrey asked.

"That's right. Each of you take a vehicle—a Ford or Chevrolet-- and register for separate rooms. Don't be seen together at the motel. Keep a low profile. When you meet, do it in a place where you won't be seen. Tell your wives that you have a mission, ordered by me. You can call them each night, so they won't worry. I'll also talk with them and assure them that your mission is important, but not dangerous."

He stood up and walked around the desk to shake each man's hand.

"Any questions, men?"

"Sir," Godfrey said, "If one of us should slip up and get arrested, should we call you?"

"First of all, Sergeant, I don't expect any of you to slip up. But if you should be arrested or have trouble of any kind, do not call me. I'll give you the telephone number of a friend of mine in Fairchance. This is extremely confidential. He works for me, and his name should not be mentioned to anyone. If you need to call him, use his code name Mr. Joe Tate."

Once they had the contact number, the three men left General Metcalf alone in his living room. They knew what to do, and he trusted them to do it well. As soon as the daily routines of their targets were determined, then the rest would be easy. He locked the door, and walked to the liquor shelves. Since he planned no activity today, it wasn't too early to have a drink of Scotch. He plopped two ice cubes into a double, took the drink to his favorite chair, and pushed back, satisfied that his best men were on the job.

As he often did, he reflected on all that he owned and what he had created in the middle of 800 wooded acres. He had bought it, built on it, gathered men and women who had the funds to join him in creating a unique town. Together, they envisioned a future that would include everything needed for a self-sustaining community. Soon there would be a real church building, a bigger clinic, and most importantly, their own bank. There would be no end to this realm, *his* realm. This was his kingdom. Twenty years ago this was only a germ of an idea. At that time, he couldn't envision the extent of its growth, never thought it would be like this. When he finally came upon this property for sale and heard what locals called it--The Kingdom--he began to dream. No one knew how a wooded area like this of fields and mountain got its name, or why, but today it was just that, a kingdom, and he was the king who ruled it.

He left the chair to replenish his drink, and then walked to the window overlooking the compound. He had time to reflect on future conquests. And he could drink as much as he wanted. He wouldn't allow the government to take away what was rightfully his. He'd worked hard to achieve his four stars when he served in the Army. They wouldn't come after him. But it wouldn't matter.

He was ready. The day would come when he and his men would go on the march. Liberation Day. It would be in his hands.

In here no one could hear him shout, "Come the Revolution!" while holding his glass high in a toast to the overthrow of the government. Patriots of the country would make it happen. There would be no laying down arms, no bending.

He never considered himself a vindictive man, but there were times when trouble had to be stopped before it had a chance to start. The Kingdom had to be safeguarded. He could tolerate no interference with his plan, the one that he alone had created and that his own troops would carry out. He had to see to it that nothing went wrong. This was where the great day would begin, right here in the heart of Maine. It would spread from here throughout the United States until the country returned to its roots, under the leadership of true Patriots.

That's why Cat Cotter must be stopped. On the other hand, Astrid Lincoln…now there was a real woman. He loved the long, lanky type, especially when they had brains. But for now, he must remember the priority.

"First, terrorize. Then, dominate."

He'd never written the slogan, but as he thought about it and took his third drink, the more he liked it. He'd love to dominate that blond Swede.

CHAPTER 21

Charlie tucked Jenny's arm in his, feeling awful pride to walk her into the Edge of Town Restaurant. To him, she was still his lovely bride and she always would be, not only beautiful in face, but especially in heart. To think that he never would have met her if he hadn't called Dee for facts those many years ago, bold and brash, seeking information about her mother's death. He'd only guessed at the truth, but it turned out to be more than he ever expected. So many years ago, but every so often he remembered the mystery surrounding Aletha's death and how he aided Dee in proving that the police were wrong, that her mother didn't commit suicide, and then the ultimate revelation of a far-reaching conspiracy.

Two waitresses looked up, and when they saw who had come in, one walked away. The couple was no stranger.

"Good evening, Charlie and Jenny."

"Good evening, Roseanne. The usual table, please."

He and Jen followed her to their special corner table.

"Are you moved in?" Roseanne asked.

"We are," Jenny said. "We got a very nice apartment on Elm Street. It's cozy."

"I have a cozy place, too, only I call it really small."

After giving their orders, Jenny said, "You can always count on Roseanne for a laugh or two. She's a nice woman."

"Oh, oh. There's Will. That must be his wife. Haven't seen her before."

"Invite them over, Dear."

Charlie hesitated. Jen gave him a nudge.

"Go ahead."

"I thought we'd have a quiet supper…"

"Oh, there'll be plenty of quiet suppers. I want to meet them."

He stood up, waved and beckoned, catching Will's attention. As they approached, Will held out his hand to Jenny.

"Hello," he said. "I'm Will. Since you're with Charlie, I expect you're Jenny."

"If not, then he's in big trouble," she said.

They all laughed. The ice was broken.

"This is my wife, Geena. We don't want to intrude on your privacy here."

Jenny said, "Not at all. Please sit with us. It's so good to meet you both."

After they settled at the table, Charlie looked at Geena.

"Did you read your husband's stories in this week's issue, Geena?"

"Actually, I haven't had a chance. I was at the hospital for a while today to see if they needed a nurse. Then I went house hunting. This is the first time Will and I have had together since early morning. We're staying here, of course. But being busy is no excuse. Last night, we did something we haven't done in years. Went to a movie. I'm afraid the paper is on the table right where he left it when he came in. And to be honest, he's so quiet about what he does that unless I probe a bit, he doesn't point out what he has written. I do know, though, that he's an excellent reporter."

Charlie liked Geena's manner, a bit like Jen's, soft spoken, soothing, no doubt comforting to her patients. Her dirty blond hair twisted into a knot gave her a plain look, but her gray/blue eyes beamed with life.

"You went to the theater here in Fairchance?" he said.

"Yes. Have you seen the movie they're playing now--*Uncle Buck*?"

Jenny said, "I've heard it's funny, but we haven't seen it."

"Well, you should, just for an evening of relaxation. It's very funny, and if you have children, you'll relate to Uncle Buck's challenge with the three he's supposed to watch while their parents are gone. I'm not a big fan of John Candy, but I did like this a lot."

"There, Charlie. Now we have to go." Jen looked at Geena again. "Well, did you get a job at the hospital?"

"Not right now, but they said there may be an opening very soon. A nurse is getting married and will be leaving."

"But we did find a house," Will said.

"Oh, good for you. Big enough for your family? I think Charlie said you have three children."

"It's big enough," Geena said. "Too big, really. Those old arks go pretty cheap these days, you know."

"Did you buy?"

"No, just renting. It's not too far from the hospital." Geena's hesitation said that she had low expectations. "Assuming we need to be near the hospital."

Their food arrived, and for a few minutes, conversation lagged. Finally, it was Will who spoke.

"Charlie, you planning to follow up on Astrid's story?"

"That's the plan after Astrid gets more legal facts."

Geena raised her eyebrows. "What's that about?" she said.

"There's a militia group out in the country," Will said,

"and Astrid went out there for an interview. Her story is in the paper—you know, the one that's on the table where you left it."

He grinned, but Geena looked a bit pained, as if she had been accused of wrongdoing.

"For now," Charlie said, "we're not saying much about it, not until Astrid has a chance to learn what the law says about it, and whether those guys are a threat. Could be just people who enjoy shooting guns."

"You know," Will said, "Astrid seemed more than a little upset by her interview with that general. You're right, of course, they may not be more than outdoors people, getting together for fun. But I have to tell you that I was in the South when I was a child. I stood and watched while a bunch of white teenagers ganged up on a black boy. They beat him savagely, and from there a small riot broke out. If you never saw a group of people go crazy and all act like one to destroy a section of town, then you're lucky. I hope this militia is an innocent group like you say, but if it isn't, if they plan on destruction, then we better hope the gendarmes are prepared to do battle."

"Oh Will," Geena said, "you're always so negative about people. We're in Maine, for heaven's sake, not the South. Nothing like that will happen here."

Charlie thought of what Astrid said while she was writing her story, "I won't use this in today's story, but General Metcalf has a swastika flag in front of his headquarters. He spoke against inferior people and implied that he believes in slavery. To tell the truth, he scares the hell out of me."

Complacency among the population, according to Cat Cotter, was exactly what hate groups and militias counted on, and Charlie wanted not to think that she could be right.

. . . .

156

Marvin held the chair for Dee. If they had been alone, he would have leaned down and kissed the top of her head, but here in the restaurant, it wouldn't be appropriate. He had noticed that she favored propriety, and that was okay with him.

When the waitress offered to light the candle on their table, Marvin said not to bother. Their end of the room was almost hidden from view of the general room by a planter. They gave their orders.

Dee said. "I really do like this restaurant. Everything is so… oh look. Charlie and Will are just leaving with their wives. They must not have seen us come in."

Marvin sat across from Dee so that he could look at her.

"Or maybe they just thought we'd like privacy," he said.

"I can't imagine why."

"You can't?"

Surely she knew how he admired her. At the office he had kissed her with passion, and she responded. He wouldn't believe that she was toying with his affections. Though she had told him how full of fire she was when she opened the rehab camp and how she'd mellowed through the years of dealing with all the problems associated with it, as well as losing her husband, she still had plenty of energy and warmth. It would take very little, he was certain, to light the fire again.

His feelings for her had soared in the past few weeks. It took a while for him to regain perspective when his beloved Rebecca died, but now his mind was made up. The Mediterranean cruise had not erased Dee from his memory, though he'd thought it might. He took the cruise to be certain, to see how absence would affect his heart. When he returned, he was almost breathless the first time he saw her again. His feelings had been sorted out.

"Marvin," Dee said, "are you trying to tell me something?"

The opening, and it came from her own lips.

"This may not be the setting I'd have chosen to say this, but I am trying to tell you something. I've tried to say this for a long time. When I'm not near you, you're in my thoughts constantly. Dee, you're the loveliest, kindest, most generous, most desirable woman in the world. You have a depth of understanding that few have."

He ran his hand through his hair and lowered his eyes. His heart raced so hard he wondered if he would have a heart attack and die while proposing.

"I feel almost tongue-tied, like a teenager asking for his first kiss. Please excuse my bungling way. What I mean to say is you have so captured my heart that I feel I can't live without you. Do you think…that is, am I out of line here?"

Dee's silence and look of surprise confused him. He *was* out of line. She was trying to think how to refuse him and not hurt his feelings. He should just get up and leave, or at most, have dinner with her and get out of her life.

"I'm overwhelmed," she said. "It sounds like you're proposing to me."

"I am. But if the idea is abhorrent to you, please just say so and I won't haunt you with repeated advances. Just…"

"Marvin. Stop. I'll marry you." She reached across the table for his hand. "I'll be so happy to marry you. I was afraid this feeling was all mine. You know, it has been a long time since I've been in love."

"In love."

He sighed. He felt like a lead bar had been lifted from his chest.

"I love you more than I can tell you," he said. "If we weren't here, and if our dinners weren't just now coming, I'd…"

He never did finish the sentence, but he didn't really need to.

CHAPTER 22

Friday morning Abram watched Astrid get dressed for work, a pleasant wake-up call, if just a bit unsettling considering that it was the wrong time of day to suggest she come back to bed.

"Busy day today?" he asked.

"You're awake. I was trying to be quiet. Ya, I'll start writing the follow-up story about the militia. Oh, I didn't get a chance to tell you last night that Cat Cotter brought in another letter. Poor woman. She is so uptight about this group. I swear, she'll have a stroke if she keeps on."

She stepped into her gray stripe pants, and Abram sighed. Show over, he sat on the side of the bed.

"I thought she had pretty well exhausted her rant about them. What's she up to now?"

"Well, oddly enough, she did bring in some information that none of us knew about. It seems that ten years ago a man by the name of Louis Beam was screaming for blood in public denunciation of the government. He headed up an organization called the Texas Emergency Reserve militia. Any other time, we might have shrugged it off as just that crazy Cat Cotter out to kill any group of men who had a love affair with weapons. But now, I'm not so sure. I think I'll go to her home and talk with her. I'd like to see the source of her information before discarding it. You know?"

She now had her jacket on and looked over at Abram with a question in her eyes, suggesting that she wanted his approval. But he knew she'd do what she wanted to. When she came over to sit beside him and give him a kiss, he noticed her ring.

"Damn," he said. "I forgot. We were going to discuss your ring. How about tonight? I go to work at two o'clock today and should be home by 10. I'll tell you then. You want me to bring home a pizza for a late-night snack?"

He was rubbing her back with enthusiasm. "Huh? What'ya say?"

She gave him another kiss.

"Sounds good to me, Honey. I have to go now, though."

"I know. I'll come down and have breakfast with you."

She got to the bedroom door and thought to say, "You could stay in bed a while longer and get a good rest."

"No, I think I can manage it. You haven't ruined me yet."

"You're so aggravating at times."

. . . .

It was 8:30 and Astrid took a chance that Cat Cotter would be up and around. She shouldn't have worried. Cat answered on the first ring.

"Yes," Cat said to the question whether they might talk at Cat's home. "I'd welcome you, Astrid. Thank you for calling."

Hanging up, Astrid said to Charlie, "I'll go interview Cat, and I'll make a call at the sheriff's office afterward, unless you have something else for me to do this morning."

"No. You go. Do whatever you need to do. This is the big story. I've saved space on page one for it."

"Good. If I can sort the facts from the hysteria, I think Cat's information will serve us well on this one."

She went to the lounge, looked out at the parking lot, but didn't see Dee's car. Rinsing out the cups at the apartment size sink, she returned to the news room and got her things to go.

"Have you seen Dee this morning?" she asked.

"No. Will and I noticed her going to dinner with Marvin last night, at the restaurant, but they went to the opposite end of the room and we didn't speak to them. It was late. We all wanted to get home."

Will said, "She wouldn't come in here anyway, would she, now that she's moved upstairs?"

"She'd check in," Charlie said. "That's her way. She'll be keeping close tabs on what goes on. You can be sure of that."

"Ya. She will. Okay. I'm off then. See you later."

Astrid found that Cat and her husband lived in a white Colonial house. Not surprising, given the neighborhood of houses in that same elegant, formal style.

Cat came to the back door wearing a pair of jeans, gray sweatshirt, and white sneakers. Astrid had pictured this old school teacher as one who would be in a dress even around the house. The one thing that still intrigued her about Cat was that wide awake, right here, right now look that challenged the world.

"Come in, Astrid. I've set us up at the dining room table. Would you like coffee?"

"No thanks. I've had more than enough already."

They went through the tidy, old-fashioned kitchen into a spacious dining room where the table was covered with papers, notebooks, and scrapbooks. Astrid presumed that the many framed photos on the buffet were family members.

"Lovely antique furnishings," Astrid said.

"You like antiques, do you?"

"Ya, We had similar things in my family home."

"These were in my family home, too. Now, let me show you some of the clippings that I have here."

"About that man Beam?"

"Louis Beam. Yes, some of them. Did you know about him and his militia?"

"No. Not until I read your letter to the editor. You must have been collecting this material for many years. I've never read much about militias myself. In fact, nothing."

"Once you start looking, you find a lot of information. It's like anything else. I enjoyed research as a student, and when I became a teacher, I insisted my classes learn how and where to get information. It's so important to everything in life."

"Ya," Astrid said, but without true conviction since she had so little time to spend on research.

"If you don't know about Louis Beam, then let me tell you a couple of things. He believes and teaches that the white race is the only race that should rule this country. In 1981, he faced a Texas federal court on charges of harassing Vietnamese fishermen in Galveston Bay. He was forced to stop that action and to disband his 2,500-member parliamentary army."

"Is he still active?"

"Oh yes. Let's see." Cat opened two scrapbooks before coming to the clipping she wanted. "See here, his group was called the Texas Emergency Reserve militia. Here, in this report he's quoted as saying, 'It's time to begin to reclaim this country for white people.' And then he says that this will be done 'the way the founding fathers got it--Blood! Blood! Blood!' Here is another quote. 'Never let any race but the white race rule this country.' You see? That was why I wrote that letter to you. Your story about the militia at The Kingdom hinted at the race issue, and I gathered they are of that mind set."

"You're right. Though it did sound to me as if General Metcalf had an even bigger agenda than a racial one. He talks wildly against the government and believes that they will confiscate all guns. He says his militia will protect the public from government's tyranny, and he also claims that all Maine counties and those in other states will form militias. He's not modest. He plans to be the commander-in-chief of all the militias."

"I believe that with all their rhetoric about an idealistic state," Cat said, "government oppression, and all the other things they hate, the militias are, in fact, all about guns. Members fear more than anything that their weapons will be taken from them. So, if there's a hint of something they don't like, a new government regulation or a tax, whatever, they can pontificate how they will protect everyone. Hate groups love their guns. With them, they have a sense of power. They can prove that they're not vulnerable when they have guns to enforce what they want."

Astrid thought of all that The Kingdom had in place.

"The general and his men and women aren't poor," she said. "They have a beautiful, well-stocked compound out in the woods. They're dressed expensively, and they have high-end vehicles. But their hate is unbelievable. One man said to me that all non-whites and Jews should be killed."

Cat looked up when her husband came into the room.

"Roy. This is Astrid Lincoln."

"Pleased to meet you, Astrid. Is Cat filling you with her anti-gun arguments?"

It was obvious that he didn't approve. And yet today Cat talked calmly, not in that excited pitch that she had when she came to the office.

"She's giving me good information about militias."

"She does have a trove of that," he said. "I'm afraid I've been a bit hard on her for all those letters she's been writing."

He appeared to be a gentle man, not very tall. His thick white hair and brown sweater with leather elbow patches gave him a scholarly, distinguished appearance. All he lacked was a pipe. Astrid thought he and Cat made a charming couple.

"We at the newspaper have a whole new perspective on her letters now that I've seen first-hand what she's talking about."

Astrid turned back to Cat.

"I mean it when I say I'm grateful for your input."

Cat smiled for the first time since Astrid came in. The change that had come over Cat was remarkable. No doubt she was relieved to have someone give credence to what had been trivialized for so long.

Roy was about to speak, but Cat interrupted him.

"Don't misunderstand me," she said. "When I say that those who join militias and other hate groups relish the power they feel with their guns, I don't mean that they are all poor. Attitude, whether it's self-confidence or inferiority, is not confined to a particular income level. Persons rich or poor live with hang-ups. Some are more able to balance their emotions than others."

Still standing behind a chair, Roy kept his eyes on Astrid, and she felt that he was studying her reaction to his wife's comments.

"That neo-Nazi antigovernment talk," Cat said, "is right out of *The Turner Diaries*."

Astrid picked up on that.

"Do you know what that book is?"

"Of course." Cat said it as if everyone in the world knew. "Don't you?"

"No. I saw a copy of it on Metcalf's coffee table. What is it?"

"See? I'm not so wrong." She looked straight at Roy. "Everyone thinks I'm crazy because I tell them about what's going on around them, but I'm not. I've studied these things."

Roy simply said, "Mmm. I know."

"*The Turner Diaries,*" she said, "was written in the late 1970s by William Luther Pierce using the pseudonym, Andrew Macdonald. It reads like a diary that starts after the government has confiscated all civilian weapons. The fictional author, Earl Turner, leaves no one out in his white supremacy outlook. It's an inflammatory, bigoted novel, a favorite for those who find nothing but fault with the government and who believe in brute strength and physical fighting as the solution to what they oppose. In what he called being at war with the System, this Turner gives day-by-day activity leading to a monumental revolution resulting in the New Era. It's all about hating what he calls the System, and isn't that familiar? He speaks of the government's Gun Raids, capitalizing those words, like a milestone event in U.S. history. Those who talk revolution love books like this, and it's particularly appealing to those who fear and hate authority. They make plans to kill government figures all the way from the president down to the lowest clerks. At the end of the book, the entire world is under this new regime, all whites, all at peace, except those that the Organization, as they call themselves, has eradicated. China, for instance, is a wasteland."

"That would be an unthinkable holocaust."

"Yes, it would. The fictional account mentions extermination of all impure groups--Jews, gay people, non-whites."

"Hard to believe that anyone could align with such thinking," Astrid said.

She tipped her head back in thought. Although Cat was considered to be crazy, just as she had remarked, or at least a bit off center, in reality she knew more than the average person, but had been dubbed whacky because of this desire to warn the public about what she saw as the danger of guns. As she considered it now, Astrid realized a flaw in the reasoning.

"Just one question," she said. "If you see the ownership of

guns so dangerous, then what would happen if the government confiscated all weapons? Wouldn't that be likely to result in a revolution, just as that book describes?"

She might as well have asked Cat what would happen if the sun stopped to shine, Cat looked so shocked.

"Well. I don't think so. The book is total fiction. If honest people understood the dangers...No, I'm right. Guns are danger-ous."

"But *are* the guns dangerous? If people are honest as you just pointed out, then can't they be trusted with guns in their posses-sion? Does a gun in the house mean the homeowner is going out to shoot everyone he or she meets? Or does a group of hunters at a hunting lodge plan an attack on the White House?"

That stopped Cat. Had she not thought about these things? As a former hunter herself, Astrid thought the question reasonable. Looking at Roy, she saw that he, too, appeared bewildered. No doubt, he'd never asked that question of his wife. Suddenly, he started for the kitchen.

"May I get you two a cup of coffee?" he asked.

"No, Roy," Cat said sharply. "I already asked Astrid."

Astrid looked at her watch.

"I do have to see the sheriff before going back to the office."

She could almost feel rays of bitterness emanating from Cat.

"If you're interested in Louis Beam," Cat said, "and more of his activity, I'll let you take this scrapbook of newspaper clippings to study. You may find one or two things to use in your story. If you still plan to pursue the story."

"Of course I do. Thank you. I'll bring this back early next week."

"Keep it as long as you need it. I presume you are going to tell us more about this General Metcalf this coming week?"

"Ya. I did leave out some important material last week, but I need to be on solid footing before I publish it. You understand."

Cat pulled herself up as tall as she could and in a stern voice said, "I have received that message myself, loud and clear. What I've written gets very little ink, as they say, but I still think guns are the problem in society today."

"I understand," Astrid said.

At the door, she took the tiny woman's hand.

"Thank you, Cat. You've been very helpful. I mean it."

. . . .

Cat watched the Jeep pull away from her driveway, then scurried to the kitchen, where Roy was reading a newspaper and drinking coffee.

"Well? What do you think now?" she asked while pouring coffee for herself.

"She's a tall girl."

"You know what I mean." Cat brought a package of Stella D'oros to the table. "These are good. Have one."

He took a cookie and bit into it.

"They're nothing but air."

"You're grumpy this morning. Did I conduct myself satisfactorily with Astrid? I gave her most of my clippings. So you won't hear me typing any more letters. If this starts the publicity that I'd hoped for, then my job is done. I'm finished trying to get newspapers and law enforcers to do something about gun controls."

Roy continued to read the newspaper.

"Nothing to say to that?" she said.

He looked over his reading glasses at her.

"If I thought you meant it, I'd dance a jig. But I know you. Something will tick you off and the next thing you'll be sending off letters trying to get something fixed. You can't live in a perfect world, Cat. If only you could just settle for what you have. Just be content that you're healthy, warm, well fed, comfortable and you can do anything you want to do, read whatever you want to read. Why don't you write a book? You could write a novel. You have the imagination. Anyway, what we have should be enough for anyone. It should be enough for you."

Cat cleared away the cups and cookies without further word on the subject.

"I'm going for my walk," she said. "Are you coming with me?"

. . . .

As she left the driveway and drove toward the Sheriff's Office, Astrid noticed the car behind her. It was the same one she'd seen earlier. Could it be that she was being followed? Was she already the target of the militia? She kept looking, first in the inside rear view mirror, and next in the outside one. Would they be so bold as to drive into the parking lot at the Sheriff's Office?

Good lord, I'm getting paranoid, of all things.

CHAPTER 23

Just before two o'clock, Abram sat in the swivel chair at the sheriff's dispatch radio, ready for work in the small room. Unusually talkative today, Freddy seemed reluctant to leave. He continued detailing the only excitement this morning...a horse, loose on Main Street. According to one of the patrolmen, the roan workhorse broke through a fence at Fairchance College.

"They had a time getting him," Freddy said. "Not many farmers working in town."

He laughed heartily at his own observation.

"Did they get him back where he belonged?" Abram asked.

"Yeah, but only after the police called the college and told them to get someone here pronto, someone who knew more about horses than they did. And...and, just after the farm manager got here and started to lead the horse toward the trailer, it lifted its tail and plopped a real big pancake in the middle of the street."

Abram grinned. "So someone had to clean that up, too."

"Oh boy. I tell you. The man who came for the horse was prepared for anything. He had a shovel and big pail. He shoveled into that steaming mess, and I heard that the air as far as the next block was filled with au-de-horsepucky."

Abram took a deputy's call, and still Freddy remained.

"So tell me," Freddy said, "how's your wife doing on that militia thing? Anything new?"

"Not that I know about. She planned to see the sheriff today. And I guess she's talking with Cat Cotter to get some information about a group in Texas. I don't know what that's all about. She'll dig up what she can, you can be sure of that."

"What she hope to do with this? I mean, they sound harmless enough, don't you think? Just guys who like to get together and do some shooting. Maybe they have a few war games, too, while they're about it, but how bad can that be?"

"That's the question. Cat Cotter doesn't think they're harmless, but that doesn't mean much. I don't think you can go by what she's saying."

Freddy laughed.

"Nope. I wouldn't say so. I think she's ready for the looney bin, myself. Everyone here does, too."

Abram took another call and dispatched a house number for a unit to investigate the report of stolen goods.

"Well, ol' boy, I'll leave you to your fun. Gotta get home to the wife and screaming kids. When are you on duty again?"

"Tomorrow, same time. Then I'm off until Wednesday morning."

"Long, long weekend. Nice going."

"Not my choice. I'd like to work full time, but I guess not yet."

"Have you made plans for your time off? You ski, don't you?"

"Astrid and I both ski, but we won't be doing that. I expect we'll shoot some pool in the rec. room. I just got it all painted. The pool table was there when we took the lease. Now she's thinking of getting a couple more things for it. She'll have something planned, I'm sure."

"Wives do that. They find a million little jobs for us. I think they don't like to see us relax for a minute."

"No doubt."

Freddy left, and Abram thought about a home with screaming kids. Freddy talked as if it were punishment. Well, maybe for him, but Abram thought it didn't have to be a problem. In fact, he hoped one day to have the same problem--a bunch of kids, screaming or not.

The afternoon and early evening hours went like any other on this job. He had time to scan a couple of magazines, but he wasn't really interested in golf and both of these were golfing magazines. A bit off-season, he thought. He'd have to bring in some of his own tomorrow. It was just after 7 o'clock, when he answered a call and heard screaming in the background. Abram came wide awake.

"Request backup and ambulance at the library. Woman has been shot."

Abram knew just what to do, and within seconds had officers and ambulance on their way to the library. Now the question was whether he should call the sheriff. He looked at the clock, and decided it would be okay at this time of night considering the serious nature of the call.

Larry himself answered on the first ring.

"This is Sheriff Knight."

"It's Abram Lincoln. A woman has been shot at the library. She's still alive. The call just came in, and I've sent officers and an ambulance. I thought you would want to know.

"Yes, of course. Thanks, Abe."

The only person in the world who called him Abe was Larry Knight. Abram never corrected him, but if any of the other men were to begin using it, he'd punch out their lights. The next step would be Honest Abe, and that would really tick him off.

When he was sure he'd done all he could, he picked up the

phone and called Astrid. She could get to the library quickly, since it was located on the other end of town, not far from Chestnut Hill Road.

"There's been a shooting at the library," he told her. "The victim's a woman."

"How long has it been?"

"Only a matter of minutes."

"Is she dead?"

"I don't think so. They called for an ambulance."

"Thanks, Dear. I'll get over there right now."

. . . .

On the way, Astrid thought, "Don't let it be Cat. Don't let it be Cat," though why she would think that was a mystery.

She found a small crowd surrounding the ambulance. Both the sheriff and the new chief of police, Jake Raleigh, stood next to the emergency workers and as she walked over to them, the wounded woman was lifted into the ambulance on a gurney.

One man said in a loud voice, "Where's the bastard who did this?"

Chief Raleigh, a rugged man who could be mistaken for a wrestler in height and girth, went to the questioner.

"We have him in custody."

"Just wanted to know that justice would be done," the man said. "She's a good woman."

"She a friend of yours?"

"Yes. She's Ellen Rand. She came to the lecture with me."

"Who are you?"

"You really need that?"

Astrid could see his agitation, and thought it strange that he should not want to cooperate.

"I need your name. If you don't want to give it to me here, we can talk at the station."

"It's Wallace Kinghorn," the man said with less sharpness. "Wally."

"How come you brought her?"

"Well…ah…I'm her neighbor, and she wanted to hear this woman's talk."

"Why didn't her husband bring her?"

"How the hell do I know? Ellen said her husband didn't want to take her, and she asked me if I would. That's all I know."

"Come with me. We'll talk at the station."

"I gave you what you asked for. I'm just the innocent neighbor. Why do you need me?"

Astrid had been snapping pictures from the time she got out of the Jeep until now.

"Hey you," Wally said. "Don't you print a picture of me in the paper. You hear me? I'll sue you personally as well as your paper if you do."

She shrugged. "Sue away," she said.

Before she left the scene, she asked the few remaining onlookers if they had seen the shooting. They all said no.

The sheriff, looking grim, emerged from the library. When he saw Astrid, he waited for her before leaving in his car.

"Sheriff," she said, "I see that you have a man in the back. Is he the shooter?"

"It's too soon to know, Astrid. What we know is that it's the woman's husband. I don't want this printed until we've had time to confirm it, but I'm pretty sure he's the shooter."

"Do you have the name of the woman who was shot, or her husband, and is she seriously hurt?"

"It appears not. All that I could see was a wound to her left arm.

You can talk with either me or Chief Raleigh or Detective Green tomorrow. We'll give you the names and more details then."

He sped off with the suspect, followed by Detective Green. Astrid went to her Jeep and sat writing notes for a few minutes before starting home. When she pulled out of the parking lot, she saw it again. That same brown car behind her.

. . . .

It was just 10:15 when Abram came through the back door. She got up from the kitchen table, kissed him, and plugged in the coffee pot.

"That will taste good, after the instant stuff I had at the office," he said. He opened the cupboard door and got two mugs. "Now, tell me about the shooting. I know the woman didn't die."

"No, the sheriff said it was an arm wound. I guess her husband didn't really want her dead. Just wanted to scare her. I expect he did that, all right."

"The late night dispatcher told me he's their neighbor. He said they fight like cats and dogs, almost every day. He said he wouldn't have been surprised if he *had* killed her."

Astrid set a plate of chocolate covered Grahams on the table.

"Looks like one of those triangles," she said. "I guess your dispatcher isn't the neighbor who took her to hear the speaker. He said his name is Wally Kinghorn. I wonder how many times they step out together. Must be some reason for the husband to take a pot shot at his wife. Surprising that it wasn't at the neighbor."

Abram poured the coffee, and they settled down to the snack before Astrid thought to ask, "Abram, have you noticed a brown car hanging around here or your office?"

"No. Why?"

"Oh nothing, I guess. It's just that I've seen one behind me three or four times now. I had the creepy feeling that I was being watched. How silly is that? I think I'm still a bit paranoid. I think I see Jimmy all over again. It's nonsense."

"I don't suppose you got a license number."

"No. Just when I catch sight of the car, he drives away on a side street, or falls behind in traffic. I never can quite make out the driver's face. I do make eye contact in the rear view mirror. That's when the car disappears somewhere. Well, just forget it. You know, if it's not imagined threats, it's real ones. That Wally Kinghorn threatened to sue me and the newspaper if I print a picture of him."

"You think that's likely?"

"No. People are always saying something like that. As if they have the money in the first place to hire an attorney. I'll worry about having an accident before I'll worry about a lawsuit. Besides, we have a very good attorney for the newspaper."

. . . .

Sergeant Norman went to a pay phone, looked all around, saw no one nearby, and dialed the number he had from the general.

"Mr. Joe Tate?" he asked when the ring was answered.

"Yes."

"Norman here. Mission completed."

"Very good."

After hanging up, Norman drove back to the motel. The three had already ended the day's surveillance, and they had talked secretly in a booth at an out-of-town tavern.

Now, in the motel dining room, each took a separate table, glanced at the other two and ate silently while reading a newspaper. They were nearly ready with their report to General Metcalf, and felt confident that they had a good plan for slowing, if not eliminating, the adverse publicity concerning their militia. They believed in a widespread militia movement, and worked every day to place ads in large circulation newspapers and to talk on short-wave radio urging those with concerns about individual freedoms to join their fight. But how soon and how extensive the fight could be remained a point of controversy.

When General Metcalf began recruiting and training at The Kingdom, he laid out a long-range plan in which this militia and those from other states would unite in the cause of exercising rights and freedoms. Now, fear had begun to spread in the militia community that the general no longer had a grip on reality, that his focus had become blurred, and that he appeared more and more angry, anxious to begin killing. He had even suggested that the state of Maine withdraw from the Union and become an independent nation. Some of the militants had already returned to their former lives in quiet towns. The future in which a swell of like-minded armies rose up in revolution appealed, but the prospect of dying prematurely to satisfy the ego of one man in a losing local fight chilled even the hardiest of dissenters.

CHAPTER 24

Saturday morning Astrid planned to sleep in. She and Abram had stayed up late to watch a late movie. But at eight a.m. the phone rang next to her ear.

"Oh for godsake," she said. "Who's that at this hour?"

In his sleep-husky voice, Abram said, "Try answering. You may find out."

She kicked sideways at his leg.

"Hello."

"Astrid. Did you hear about the shooting last night? It was at the library. It's them. I know it is. They're here in Fairchance. We need to get prepared. Talk with the police. Tell them."

"Cat? What are you talking about?"

"The shooting last night. At the library. Didn't you hear about it?"

"Ya. I was there. The woman was shot by her husband. She only has a flesh wound. Nothing serious."

"Oh? You mean…? I thought…Well, that's how it will start, you know. One of the militia men will shoot someone, and another, and another. They'll begin terrorizing us all."

Astrid rolled her eyes at Abram, who was now putting on his robe to go downstairs.

"Cat, please calm down. There's nothing to worry about. This was a domestic dispute that ended up badly. That's all it was. And the militia will not be shooting us one by one, I assure you. Now, take it easy."

"I suppose. Well." Astrid could hear the harrumph in her voice. "I'm sorry I bothered you."

"It's no bother. Try to relax. I'll talk with you another day. Okay?"

"Okay."

"I guess we're up," Astrid said when she finished. "Nothing like an early morning phone call from Cat Cotter. She's as wild as ever."

"What did she want? Worried that the militia was invading?"

"Ya. That's it."

Astrid soon had her robe on, and they walked downstairs to have breakfast.

"Maybe she's right," Abram said. "Maybe they will attack. But I think they'd blow up some building rather than shoot individuals. Buildings can't shoot back."

They began setting up for breakfast. When Abram said that, Astrid hesitated. He'd made a cogent, disturbing point.

"You could be right. I wonder what building they would explode."

"Something to send a clear message. Like maybe the Post Office."

"Or maybe the court house? Or maybe *The Bugle* office."

Abram said nothing, but a look of fear crossed his face. Astrid wished she hadn't said that.

"I'm sure they're not going to do that," she said.

They finished their breakfast, but remained at the table.

"Astrid, we managed to forget the ring again last night. I should have told you about it long before now," Abram said.

"Ya. I want to hear it."

"Understand, when Gunnar came here for the wedding, I didn't yet have a wedding ring for you."

Abram explained how Gunnar had brought the ring to him and insisted that he use it as his wedding ring. He went on with the story as Gunnar had told him.

"I wanted to refuse it," he concluded. "But I didn't want to hurt Gunnar's feelings when he'd been so considerate to bring it."

"Ya. Very considerate. Especially since it had a curse attached. I can just see Gunnar afterward, grinning with satisfaction that he put something over on his sister. Well, on you, too, but especially me."

"I was hoping you wouldn't get upset about it. No jewelry can actually have a curse, you know."

"Oh? Then why have you been saying 'damned ring' so much? Is it because you don't believe in the curse?"

Abram remained mute, looked away as if he were trying to decide whether to be honest and say he did believe it or to say he didn't.

"I hope you're not mad," he said.

"Not mad, just hurt that you would conspire with Gunnar and then lie to me. You told me that it was your great aunt's ring."

"I didn't say that. You assumed it was my relative, but I didn't say it was. I just said it was a great aunt's ring."

"You're splitting hairs. You knew I'd believe it was your relative. I would never have thought that you'd have *my* relative's ring. I didn't even know there was one."

"That's what Gunnar said. He told me that when your grandfather was ill, he showed it to Gunnar while you were still in New York State. That was when he heard the story about the curse. He said that was when your grandfather gave it to him, and he didn't tell you about it. I guess he thought Gunnar might need money some day and could sell it."

Astrid saw the pain in Abram's face and felt sorry that he believed he'd done a terrible thing. She needed to soften her tone.

"Well, I guess that was fair enough. I got so much, and it was only right that Gunnar had something like that. Obviously no one would think I'd ever want it, not being one to wear jewelry. But I wonder why he didn't use it for his wedding."

"He told me that Charlotte wouldn't want an old ring. She preferred new."

"Ha. I can believe that. She's nothing if not a spendthrift."

She reached for Abram's hand and squeezed.

"It's okay, Honey. The truth of the matter is that I wouldn't give this ring up for anything. It's beautiful, and even if Gunnar did give it to us, it means just as much to me as if you had gone out and bought it."

"That's a relief. Maybe someday I can get one for you that's all from me."

"Don't do that. This is my ring now. Just one thing, though."

"What's that?"

"Please don't blame the ring for everything that goes wrong. Okay?"

"You bet." He leaned toward her with that devilish grin she knew so well. "I'll just blame you."

Her squeeze turned to a slap on the back of his hand.

. . . .

Cat felt like a fool. Why did she call Astrid? Of course she knew about the shooting. She'd know about any shooting in town. It was the wrong thing to do, and Monday she would apologize. Maybe if she had told Astrid about that strange car that was following her, it would have changed her mind and given her pause to consider that the militia could already be on the move for trouble. Then, again, maybe Astrid wasn't as eager as she had thought to expose the group for what it was. Those questions and comments about guns sounded like she had changed her mind about following up on this militia problem.

Roy walked in dressed for outdoors.

"Ready for our walk?" he asked.

"Ready. Just need to put boots and coat on.

"Who were you talking to?"

"Just called to see how Hilda is doing."

"Hilda?"

"She's no one you know. She's my hairdresser. Just had a baby."

He got her coat from the closet and held it for her. As she slipped her arms into the sleeves, he kissed her cheek.

"Well, you look great to me the way you are. And have I told you that I like the way you are now, all settled down, back to normal. It will be good to see everyone together for a change."

Let him think what he would. Cat knew nothing was normal. Nothing was as it seemed to be. She knew someone was following her, spying on her every move. But she wouldn't tell Roy. She liked having him be normal even if she couldn't be.

CHAPTER 25

Monday morning Astrid nearly ran into Dee and Marvin in her haste to get to work. Since there was only one other vehicle in the lot, it appeared that they had arrived together. From the broad smiles on their faces and the fact that they were holding hands, it also appeared that something beyond the newspaper was on their minds.

"Good morning, Astrid," Dee said. "Did you have a good weekend?"

"Ya, very good, thank you."

Maybe they weren't embarrassed, but Astrid felt like turning around and running to her Jeep.

"Before you get any more red-faced," Marvin said, "let me tell you why Dee and I arrived together, and if you thought we might have spent the night together, then you thought right. You see, we became engaged this weekend."

"Oh my God," Astrid blurted before she thought. Now she was more embarrassed than before at his forthright admission of a night together. "I mean, congratulations. I didn't know anything like this was going on. I mean, gee, I hope you'll be very happy together."

"Thank you, Astrid. I'm sure we will," Dee said.

"What about the others? Will you tell everyone?"

"Yes, of course. We have nothing to hide."

"We should give you a party."

Marvin shook his head.

"No need to do that. When we tie the knot, we'll throw a big bash for everyone."

"Have you set a date for the wedding?"

Dee said, "I want to have a spring wedding, perhaps late May or early June."

"That's a nice time of year. Well, I'd better get to work. Again, congratulations. I'm happy for you."

Dee went with Marvin to his office, and Astrid continued toward the editorial room, pondering that sudden announcement. Everyone knew they liked each other, but no one ever spoke of a possible marriage. As if that mattered. For one, she now believed in marriage, even when things were a bit rough. Independence had its drawbacks.

Opening the door, she stopped, listened, waited before turning on the light. She'd heard a noise. In the semi-darkness she could see a figure in black at her desk.

"What are you doing?" she said.

Without a word, he ran toward her, flashed a strong light in her eyes, and landed a punch to her mid-section. She gasped for breath, heard him running down the hallway and out the back door.

When she regained breath, she ran to the door, but he was nowhere to be seen in the parking lot. She walked back to the office, turned on the light, and sat in her chair to assess what the intruder had been looking for. At first, it appeared that nothing was missing, but then she remembered. She had left her notebook here, the one with notes from her discussion with Cat Cotter. It was gone. It was of no consequence, since she had a more reliable account of it all on her tape recorder, and that was in her bag.

She made notes along with the taping to highlight points she particularly wanted to find on the tape.

"Why would he want those?" she said aloud.

"Who wants what?"

Charlie had arrived without her noticing. He shed his winter clothes, hung them in the closet and sat at his desk.

"I didn't hear you come in," Astrid said. "When I opened the office door a few minutes ago someone was in here. He came at me flashing a light in my eyes. He punched me and got away. I would have stopped him, but he got me in the solar plexus. I couldn't breathe for a few seconds. By the time I got to the door, he was gone. I had no idea where he went, so I couldn't very well go after him."

"Well, sure, because of course you'd want to tackle a man who just might have a gun as well as the flashlight."

"You sound like Abram."

"He's sensible, too, huh?"

"You really do sound like him. Anyway, he got away with just one thing as far as I can see--my notepad with notes from the Cat Cotter interview. I was just saying I wonder what he wants with them."

"You couldn't see who it was?"

"No. I didn't turn on the light because I heard a little noise when I came in. Damn. I wish I had tripped him or something."

"Did the notepad have anything else besides that one interview?"

"No. That's all. But I have the tape recording anyway. I can't imagine why the interest."

She plugged the earphones into her tape recorder and began to listen to the interview. Then she stopped it.

"Charlie, did you ever hear of *The Turner Diaries?*"

"I don't think so. Something I should have read in high school?"

"Hardly. It shouldn't be required reading anywhere. It's the worst kind of bigoted novel. General Metcalf had one on his coffee table and it looked like it was quite worn from use."

"And?"

"Well, Cat Cotter said it proves that the militia at The Kingdom is up to no good. She says that book outlines work and plans of hate groups. But her arguments about guns fell apart."

She gave Charlie a brief description of the book as she recalled it from Cat.

"So, based on that book, I asked her if it might not be that the government would cause a revolution by those types should they confiscate guns entirely. Apparently that's how the *Diaries* novel begins--with confiscation of all guns. You see?"

"I think so. If Joe Blow had to give up his guns, he'd fight."

"Ya."

"And how would he do that without weapons?"

"My guess is that militia like General Metcalf's would dig out their hidden guns. They are also capable of making bombs, I was told."

"Sounds reasonable. Anyway, why even consider the possibility since there's no suggestion from on high that guns will be taken away."

"No, but Cat has been trying to gain support for her belief that doing away with guns would stop the killings. Her anti-gun war was waged after her brother was killed by a shooter in Boston, you know. They never found the killer nor did they know why he singled out her brother. It's presumed that it was just a drive-by, random shooting. Now she thinks these militia types will bring guns into town and start picking off people, just that same way."

"For what purpose? Still sounds crazy to me. If people want to kill, they'll find a way with or without guns. There are other weapons, like knives, poisons, or just simply hands, for that matter.

Maybe they should chop off all hands, then there would really be fewer killings."

"Oh Charlie. Come on now."

They were interrupted when Will came through the door, cheeks rosy from the cold wind.

"Did you walk?" Charlie asked.

"Yeah. It's cold, but I like it."

"Go get warmed up in the lounge. You can make the coffee."

As Astrid wrote her story, she was struck by the fact that this threesome was the whole reporting team now. No more women for her to chat with or go out to lunch with. But she didn't care. These two men were her kind of people, up for a joke, or on the run for a story, and that made her feel right at home. She always did relate to men in a working environment.

. . . .

Abram was about to get dressed when the phone rang. To his surprise it was Freddy, sounding a bit out of breath.

"Abram, I need a favor. I need someone to cover for me for about three hours this morning. Can you come in? I'd like to keep this low-key. I'll pay you my morning wages, if you will do it."

"Ahh, well, sure. I can be there in 20 minutes."

"Good. Thanks, pal. I owe you."

It was just 20 minutes later that Abram got to the dispatch office, having sneaked in by the side door, as Freddy directed.

"Good. I wouldn't ask this, but it's an emergency," Freddy said. He was already in coat and hat, headed for the door.

"No one sick, I hope."

"No. Nothing like that."

And he was gone, leaving Abram to wonder what was so important that he hadn't just asked for a substitute to come in today. He had plenty of sick leave coming.

CHAPTER 26

Monday at ten o'clock, General Metcalf stood behind his leather-top desk facing his three soldiers. Also with them was the man known only to himself. The general had never lacked ego, but ever since he talked with Astrid Lincoln he felt a heightened sense of immortality, endowed with super human strength and wisdom.

Astrid had infected him with inspiration for this transformation from preparation to action. It was time for something extraordinary to happen, something he himself would direct and that he would outline today. Now was the hour for serious talk about taking a stance, one so big that it would be written about by major newspapers and talked about on all the networks. Dressed in full uniform, displaying his medals, he looked down on the seated group.

"Men, we face serious issues today. This will be no ordinary discussion of regimental maneuvers, but rather an out-and-out collaboration for a military offensive. Before we get into details, however, I will introduce you to a man you know as Mr. Joe Tate, your Fairchance contact. Freddy, meet the three you've talked with this past week, Lieutenant Frye, Sergeant Godfrey, and Sergeant

Norman. Freddy works for the sheriff as a dispatcher, a most advantageous position for us."

Each man stood and shook Freddy's hand, then sat down for the debriefing.

"I trust all went well this past week. I'll hear from each of you before I tell you of a new development. We'll start with you, Lieutenant Frye."

Frye stood and saluted. The general trusted him the least. He was a weak man compared to the others. But he had above average intelligence, an asset no one would ever guess by those hawkish eyes.

"Abram Lincoln has a predictable schedule. I watched the house, and followed him to work each day that he worked. Two days now he has remained home, and I didn't see him leave. With binoculars one day, I observed that he went to one of his garages, left the door open, and stirred paint, so I concluded that he was painting inside the house. He would be an easy target at home. My instructions were to take no action until we agreed on how to proceed."

The general nodded. "He sounds like a dull man," he said, certain that no one understood his satisfaction in saying that.

"You could say that, Sir."

"Let's hear from you, Sergeant Godfrey. You were watching Cat Cotter."

Godfrey was the opposite of the lieutenant. He had movie star quality, handsome face and muscular body development. Of all his men, the general admired Godfrey most, believing him to be totally loyal to himself and the cause.

"Yes Sir. She moves about a good deal. I watched her at home from a distance, and followed her in the car. She shops about every day, walks with her husband every day for about an hour beginning at 10 or 10:30 in the morning. She mails letters at the post office quite often, but I couldn't get close enough to ascertain where they were sent. The couple went to the movies on Friday evening. They entertain little. She went to the library two afternoons in the week, Tuesday and Friday. And she went to the bank on Friday also, on her way to the library."

"Very good. Now Sergeant Norman, you watched Astrid Lincoln."

Norman came aboard only three months ago, and though he showed no real passion for anything, the general had immediately felt a bond transcending the listless eyes. Here was a man who would fight to the death, no question.

"Yes Sir. Because of her work, she is also active outside the home and office. I observed her at the Sheriff's Office twice, but I can't determine if that is a regular habit. There were occasional visits to offices and one to the elementary school. She was at Cat Cotter's house for about a half hour on Friday. Habitual moves seem to be from home to office early each day with a stop at the supermarket where she apparently picks up lunch items for the office, and she went to the bank on Friday at noontime. She was at the Post Office on Wednesday. She saw me in her Jeep mirrors a couple of times, but I took a side street as soon as that happened. I don't think she ever turned the Jeep around to try to find me."

"Freddy. You went to her office this morning. What did you find?"

Freddy, the family man, had come to him desperately in need of added income, heard about the militia and offered to work part-time at just about anything that was needed. He found the concept of a home militia worthwhile, he said then, and when the general told him what he needed, Freddy agreed. He would be a mole in the Sheriff's Office. He'd lived up to his assignment satisfactorily, giving the general no cause for distrust.

"I got her notebook, Sir. The one where she wrote notes from that interview she had with Cat Cotter. She walked in on me while I was searching the office, but didn't turn on the light, and I managed to give her a punch on my way out the door, so she didn't follow me out. I didn't park in their lot. Went next door and parked on the street. Of course, Abram is working part-time at the Sheriff's Office, and takes over for me. He wasn't very helpful. I tried to get information from him about his wife and the Cotter woman, but he never knew much."

"Anything significant in her notes?"

"Nothing much, except mention of *The Turner Diaries.* Nothing more on it. My guess is that she taped the interview. She doesn't have enough in her notes to write a story, unless she keeps it all in her head."

General Metcalf said, "I doubt that. You all knew what you were to do, and it sounds like you did your surveillance well."

He paced for several seconds, rubbing his chin, gathering his thoughts.

"As providence would have it," he said, "the Sunday newspaper carries a story about the governor. It seems that he is visiting all of Maine's county seats. Sunday afternoon, he will be in Fairchance. Ah, I can see you're ahead of me. What better time to send the message to all media and politicians that we're a force to be reckoned with against tyranny. We, the Patriots, will control the destiny of this country, from towns and cities to states, on to Washington, and finally, the world."

He stood straighter, savoring the moment that he could finally call for an attack.

"Men, you are about to launch the revolution. We are ready, and we have the opportunity. We could attack in a larger city, like Bangor or Augusta, but we're here and have our weapons here, should we need to defend the post. I expect you to call in all the men who have prepared for this day. We won't wait. We'll make an impression that won't soon be forgotten. Having a visit from the governor of the state is perfect. When we attack, the world will learn about the Patriots and what we represent. Freedom! That's our motto. We mustn't wait. There's no time to wait."

"Sir."

"Lieutenant Frye?"

"Surely you're not suggesting hand-to-hand combat at this early date. We may be ready, but our numbers are few. Even if we can attack that small gathering and should we manage to get out and return here, they will know us. They could go so far as to destroy the compound. Your plan has always been to use commando tactics when we do anything. Wouldn't an open attack expose us too soon, before we have allies elsewhere?"

The general ground his teeth. He wouldn't bow to Frye's reasoning. This time it would be an all out attack or nothing. He had waited for just such an opportunity, and it was here. For years he had been planning a big offensive. There was no stopping now.

"No, I don't believe we'll fail. A good offensive, a comprehensive attack leaving no witnesses, will assure us of victory. We expected to fight in this revolution, not to sit back and say we are too weak."

The lieutenant, in that insufferable tone of superior intelligence that the general disliked, stood to articulate his position. General Metcalf clenched both fists. How he wished he had refused to take this man under his command. There were signs, even then, that he would be trouble.

"The bare fact of it, Sir, is that we are *not* ready, the state of Maine is not ready with militias, nor are any bordering states. To attack the governor and innocent citizens who turn out to hear him would be to invite death to us all. We are alone. What the future holds is another matter. Maybe in time a large scale attack on a government building or officials will be within our scope of preparedness. But now, we just are not ready."

General Metcalf was ready to shoot this rebel. When he gave a command, he expected it to be carried out.

"The citizens are lazy, stupid people. They'll be there to find out what they can get from this man. I've trained you all. I know you're ready. If nothing else, we can bomb City Hall. We *are* ready."

"Not for a major attack," Frye insisted. "Maybe a sniper could get in and out without detection, but it is my belief that we should not attempt a large-scale offensive. Besides being foolhardy, it contradicts our principle of being here to protect the public. You yourself often say that the enemy is the state. Why then, this prematurely, would we kill innocent people? We should be gaining their trust, not attacking them."

Telling himself to control his temper, the general went to the window, clasped his hands behind his back, took deep breaths. Mentally, he saw guns blazing, people dropping, blood flowing in his surge on City Hall. How else could he get the message out there that he was in charge? He was the general. This was his army. He would defy the System. And he would do it now.

All right, if that was the way his own men felt about it, then he alone would be the one to make the big statement. He would accomplish what everyone seemed to think was not doable. He returned to the desk, looked each man, one-by-one, in the eyes, scowling in contempt, and gave them his final word.

"I will have no need for any of you in this operation. It will be mine alone. I trust that you can conduct day-to-day maneuvers here as usual. I'll go to Fairchance this week. I'll set up a strategy. I thought I could count on you, especially you three, to lead an offensive that would strengthen our message. But if not, then I alone will carry it out."

Each man bowed his head and looked down. Already they were the epitome of dejection, not the proud soldiers he had trained. Disgraceful.

"What's the matter? Have you gone all weak and womanly? Are you suddenly afraid of going into battle? Have all these months and years of preparation come to this? I have a spineless bunch of weaklings for an army. I'm the only man here who sees the big picture."

He swept his hand wide as he spoke those words.

"I see the day when the System will crumble, when we of the Organization will accomplish what was mapped out for us by Earl Turner. If you cannot capture the vision for the survival of our race, then you, too, will fall. I will conquer. You're either with me or against me. It is only a matter of time before we have a nationwide movement. When we are at full strength, we'll take control of an atomic bomb and clean out the devil's disciples."

He watched as each man, not looking at him, silently walked to the door and out of his presence.

"Go, then!" he shouted. "Go! You will be the losers. I'll see to that."

Freddy ran to his car and headed back toward Fairchance. At first, the militia and its goal of protection for the average citizen against an attack from within or beyond this country had sounded almost attractive to him. Now he saw a mad man, as mad as Hitler himself, who planned to annihilate life as he knew it. This mustn't happen.

"He's crazy. How can I stop this scheme of his?"

At the same time the other three gathered in Frye's house. He was the only unmarried man in the militia, and they could talk in secret here. Though he wasn't greatly admired by the others, Frye was the most capable of putting everything into perspective.

"So much for a week of surveillance," Frye said. "It's as I feared.

Metcalf has become so associated with that crazy novel that he now thinks there really was an Earl Turner. It's my guess that he'll take out himself as well as many others Sunday. I don't think he's sound enough to realize what he's doing. He plans to prove to the world that his movement toward active militias nationwide will materialize. He hates with passion, hates everything and everyone from the banking community to Congress to the president. I don't disagree with returning the country to what our founders framed in the Constitution, but he's talking death to innocents long before United Patriots are ready."

His fireplace was still burning brightly, and they stood around it to warm their hands.

"Does anyone have a suggestion how to deal with this?" he asked.

Norman said, "I think I can deal with it better if I have a drink."

"Come on out to the kitchen," Frye said. "I think we can all use a drink. We'll reconnoiter over a beer."

CHAPTER 27

After Charlie read her story, Astrid wanted Dee to look at it before sending it to page make-up. In her mind, Dee had a remarkable insight, having been through difficult experiences and many years of counseling alcoholics. Maybe that had nothing to do with being a good reporter, but Astrid would yield to her insight any day.

Running upstairs, she rapped on the door, and opened it.

"Got a couple of minutes?" she asked.

At her desk, positioned in the dormer so that she could see the door as well as down the street, Dee beckoned Astrid to come in.

"Of course. Any time, Astrid. What's up?"

The gold and beige guest chair was pretty enough to be in a living room, and it was comfortable.

"I hope you have the time to read my second story about the militia. It's filed under Militia, if you want to bring it up."

"Sure thing. I just turned on my computer. Let's see now."

When she had it, Dee said, "Is this the last of the reports, or will you go on for a longer series?"

"I'm not sure. It may be that General Metcalf will react to it, in which case, it could lead to another story. But we'll see."

As Dee read the copy, she made little throat noises which meant to Astrid that she found it disturbing.

"This Louis Beam," Dee said, "is a real bigot."

"A white supremacist in the extreme. Cat Cotter loaned me her collection of news clippings about him and his followers, and I found references to other hate groups. The more I talked with General Metcalf, the more I've come to believe he runs a radical hate group. He didn't exactly admit being neo-Nazi, but the flag and his rhetoric left me with a distinct impression that's the case. I kept hearing racist talk throughout the ranks."

Dee agreed. "Does he really think there will be groups like his all over the country in the future?"

"That's what he claims. I can't believe the overall attitude of these people. They aren't just complaining about this or that thing that the government has done. They see the whole democratic structure flawed."

"Do you think the section you wrote about the FBI in all of this should be brought up to the lead? Let the public know up front that attention is being paid to terrorism and talk of it. You mentioned it last week, but since you've written so much more detail this week about the menace of similar groups elsewhere, it seems to me that point should be emphasized. We don't want to lull the public into complacency, but on the other hand, we wouldn't want to spread fear, either. Maybe, after some sword rattling, the general and his underlings will turn out to be no more than disgruntled citizens who feel it's their duty to be prepared for the worst that could come, under what they perceive as a less than adequate government."

She thought for a couple more minutes and added, "Once you've established that they are under the watchful eye of the law, you might say something like, 'Elsewhere, similar groups have run amok with the law when they practiced illegal acts' and continue on with your researched material. What do you think?"

"That's good. I could compare the general's statements with similar statements of hate groups actively engaged in types of sabotage."

Astrid was ready to leave, but Dee had more to say.

"Your sidebar on the Posse Comitatus is interesting. I've heard of it, of course, but didn't really know much about it."

"If it ever really took hold," Astrid said, "I'm afraid a good many sheriffs would be hanged if they didn't do their duty as the organization sees it. Can you imagine having county rule instead of federal?"

"Interesting," Dee said. "Unrest and protests starting back in the 1940s. I wonder how they came by the name Silver Shirts?"

"I wonder how people who oppose paying taxes think services would be paid for without tax money. Sheriff Knight said among the things they checked concerning Metcalf's group was whether they paid taxes."

"Do they?"

"Ya. That's another thing that backs up their claim of operating legally."

"Well, you're doing a good job, Astrid. Go for it."

"Thanks. I appreciate your suggestions."

She went back to the editorial room and quickly revised her story. Charlie was looking up a word in *Roget's Thesaurus* and Will was studying the Bangor newspaper, looking for anything that could be used locally.

"Here's something," he said, "Did you get a notice on this, Charlie? About the visit our governor is making to Fairchance Sunday?"

"Yeah. I wrote a it up for a box on page one."

"Will we all cover it?"

"I don't think it's necessary. I'll cover it, but anyone can go, of course. A few extra photos wouldn't hurt. So take a camera if you do attend."

"I'll be going," Astrid said. "I've met Governor Monohan. I'd like to see him again."

"I hope he brings Taylor," Will said.

"It's a bit early for that," Charlie said. "Later, we'll see his wife when the campaign heats up. He's not doing well in the polls now, though."

"That's my point. He should bring his bride along. Sure couldn't hurt his chances."

Conversation stopped when the door opened, and Cat Cotter walked in, wrapped up against the winter cold as usual. She went to Astrid's desk.

"I came over to apologize for calling you yesterday," she said. "I hope I didn't wake you up. Roy said you might have been sleeping in on a Sunday."

"No, of course not," Astrid lied. "It's all right, Cat."

"Did you hear about the governor? He's coming here next Sunday. They'd better have protection for that young man. It could be just the venue the outlaws have been waiting for, you know. Who knows what they're planning. Maybe they'll blow up City Hall."

"I hardly think that," Astrid said.

The two men gave each other significant looks behind Cat's back. Astrid thought how too bad that everyone still thought of Cat as being crazy, and how difficult it was for her, or anyone for that matter, to have a conviction if it didn't conform to public consensus.

"I'll be going to hear him speak, Cat," she said. "Want to go with me? Or are you and Roy going together?"

"No we're not. He doesn't care for politics. I'd love to go with you."

"What time is he coming here, Charlie?"Astrid said.

"He'll come from Bangor, and should be speaking about two o'clock. But they seldom run on time."

"I'll pick you up before two, then," Astrid said to Cat.

"I'll be ready." She started for the door. "Thank you, Astrid."

After she was gone, Charlie said, "You'd better stand well back, Astrid. If City Hall goes up, you don't want to be too close."

"Ya. I'll remember that good advice. Maybe you should just get a speech handout and leave."

"If the building blows up you can say, 'I told you so.'"

"If you're in it and it blows up, which piece of you should I say that to?"

Will laughed. "Now you're getting grisly."

"Ya? Well, Cat Cotter may be a bit overly enthusiastic in her crusade against guns, but she got it right about the militia. I wish she didn't confine the threat to guns only. I think that isn't all of it."

"I like to hunt," Charlie said. "I say it's not guns but people who kill."

"Ya. I was a hunter myself. That's just one part of the problem, isn't it? I don't know how you keep crazies from killing, guns or no guns. I just don't know. For instance, blowing up a building doesn't involve a gun. I think Cat doesn't see the whole picture. The nature of man--and I do mean man--is to fight and to injure or kill others. How do you change that?"

. . . .

Abram had the table set and something baking in the oven when Astrid arrived home. Her open-mouth amazement was for real.

"Abram! What a wonderful surprise. I didn't know you could cook. What smells so good?"

"It's pot roast. I did eat before I married you, and that called for cooking or eating only sandwiches. I got tired of sandwiches."

"Well, who knew you were more than just a pretty face?"

She suppressed a gasp as she looked around at the wreck he'd created on countertops in making dinner. However, to have the meal ready when she got home after her busiest day of the week compensated for the clean-up she'd have to do.

She went to the sink and washed her hands, then gave him a kiss on the cheek.

"Thank you, Abram. I don't know anyone else whose husband cooks."

"Let's face it, you're one lucky broad."

"Oh ya. I'm hungry. Let's eat."

"Such a romantic," he said.

. . . .

Dinner over, kitchen spotless, the two sat in the den, each with a book in hand.

"Did you finish your story about the militia?" Abram said.

"Uh huh. It starts on page one tomorrow."

"So Cat Cotter had good information for you?"

"She was a wealth of information. Her husband doesn't approve of her controversial letters. You can hardly blame him. But he's nice. I'm going to take her to City Hall on Sunday to hear Governor Monohan."

"I read that the governor's coming here."

She nodded.

"I wish you could come," she said. "Do you know if you have to work?"

"Oh, I didn't tell you. Yes. I just got final approval for full-time work, beginning on Sunday. I'll be on the noon to eight shift. Not bad. Of course, it means I won't be making a feast for you each night."

"I ate before we were married, too. I think I can cope. I'm so glad for you."

She could have added that she never became as good a cook as he did, however, but she was certain he knew that already.

"Getting a good raise, too. I'll be pulling my own weight for a change."

Astrid didn't reply. His injury and long recuperation period had hurt his pride. She no longer tried to convince him that it was all right that she had taken care of him during that time.

She looked at her ring. Its beauty never ceased to please her.

"You haven't mentioned the ring lately," she said. "Did you finally decide that it couldn't have had anything to do with our streak of bad luck?"

"Well, I suppose I never did believe that. It was just an easy thing to blame. You know what I mean. A little like you blaming me for everything."

"Abram! That's not true."

"See? It just ain't so."

He could be such an aggravation at times.

CHAPTER 28

As she often did, Astrid left the office Wednesday afternoon to shop and do chores at home. On the way home, she stopped at the shoe store and bought a new pair of Dockers. From there she paid the light bill and shopped for groceries, both at the supermarket, then drove home. She had just started up the stairs to change the bed after putting away groceries, when the doorbell rang. She ran back down and looked through the frosty glass on the front door.

The sight of red hair sent a chill down her back. What did General Metcalf want and why did he come here? A telephone call at work would be more appropriate. To say the least, she could hang up on him there if he started ranting about her story. Well, one thing for sure, she would not back down to the man. She would feel easier if Abram were home.

"General Metcalf," she said on opening the door. "What brings you to my home?"

In black overcoat, he looked as if he were ready to attend a funeral. Strange not to see him in uniform.

"I thought that since you came to my home, I might be welcome in yours, as well."

Welcome in her home? Hardly. Nevertheless, she opened the door wider and swept her hand toward the living room.

"Ya. Of course. Come in. I'm surprised that you knew where to find me."

"People aren't hard to find, even out in the country."

He removed his overcoat as he entered the living room. Astrid didn't offer to hang it in the closet.

"Outstanding house," he said. "Ah, and a fireplace. Nothing like a warm fire on a cold winter day."

"Ya. I don't have one going today, though."

He walked around looking at the various paintings, picked up and examined an antique Carnival glass fruit bowl.

"Northwood. This is very valuable."

"You know antiques?"

"I enjoy fine things in life." He tilted his head toward her. "Antiques, cars, old guns."

With suggestive half-closed eyes poring into hers, he added, "And beautiful women."

What the hell…?

He threw his coat over the arm of one chair and sat in the other at the right of the fireplace. In dark navy suit, white shirt, and light blue tie, he could have been an executive, ready for a day at the office.

Astrid decided she should show a bit of hospitality, even if she felt like asking him to leave.

"May I get you something to drink? Coffee, tea?"

"No, thanks. I'm not here for a tea party."

"No? What then?"

She sat facing him, on the other side of the fireplace.

"Most direct," he said. "You know, that was what I liked about you when we talked before. I think you are one of the most direct, most interesting women I've ever known. I really wish you'd join us."

She automatically placed her right hand over the wedding ring.

"Like I said before, General, the militia isn't my kind of thing. I should have thought you would know that by the article I wrote this week, if nothing else."

"There, see?" He laughed as if he had made an important point. "You're right to the point and honest. I like that. I really like that."

She waited for what else he had to say. So far, he had managed to excite her anger, and nothing else. Either this was a whole lot of baloney leading up to some insult to make her feel small, or he was openly hitting on her.

"So you understand, I'm sure, that I don't wish to play games," she said. "If *you* have a point, will you please make it?"

Again he laughed.

"I love it," he said. "That straight to the gut punch. Well, my dear, I do have a point. You made some pretty strong statements in your story this week."

Here it comes. I'm about to be crucified.

She raised her chin, ready for whatever he had to offer.

"I won't say they're accusations. You didn't do that, at least not about us. You're a good reporter, good at digging out historical facts. And they were all accurate. I don't refute any of the report."

"You don't?"

"No. Did you think I would? Not at all. I'm here to thank you. I couldn't buy that kind of advertising. You quoted me truthfully. Already I've received visits from two men interested in joining us. They both agree with our cause. They're ready to take up arms against tyranny. They recognize the value of training for the time when every able bodied man will have to fight to restore U.S. sovereignty as proclaimed by the country's founders."

Astrid heard him, but needed a moment to understand. This approach was almost as unsettling as if he'd cast a barrage of reasons why she should retract parts of the story.

"But I didn't sugar coat the consequences of seditious acts. Louis Beam, for instance. He wants to purge the United States of all non-whites. He wanted to create his own state in Texas, and give all minorities 24 hours to leave, or they'd be exterminated. He's been charged with blowing up a couple of buildings and other acts against humanity including false imprisonment."

"I knew about Beam long before you wrote about him. But, you see, most charges against him were dropped. They can put out flames, but they can't stop the fire that travels underground."

"Those who commit capital crimes will be dealt with for what they are, whether killers or traitors, or both."

"So they say."

Astrid waited. It was obvious that he was thinking how to approach another topic, and finally he came to it.

"You mentioned *The Turner Diaries*. Have you read the book?"

"No," she said. "Cat Cotter told me about it."

"Mmm. Cat Cotter. I suppose she considers herself an expert on its message. She tell you how it ends after Patriots waged a successful revolution, and changed the world? Did she mention that the revolution extended throughout the world, and ended in peace and prosperity around the world?"

"Not quite like that."

"No. She wouldn't admit that men and women working in a great underground movement for the revolution could bring world-wide peace to all whites."

There it was. All whites. Astrid felt her anger growing.

"To be honest, General, I didn't get the impression that you were quite that extreme. You told me that the militia's primary purpose is to be prepared to aid society, not annihilate certain ones. I know you have a copy of that Turner book on your coffee table, but I didn't think you would include terrorism and genocide in your agenda. So I never said as much in my story. I pointed out that there are paranoid hate groups who *would,* though. Their paranoia goes to the extreme, while I took you to be honest and sincere in a desire to protect."

She watched him as he studied the checkered, blackened fireplace logs. What was he thinking? Would he admit the worst to her? Would he say that he was preparing his militia for revolution? Surely a reasonable, intelligent man should see the folly in such plans.

"It's a pretty fireplace," he said at last. "Are you a homebody, Astrid?"

"Am I what?"

"A homebody. Do you enjoy fire and hearth and husband at night, or do you prefer going out for a good time?"

"I enjoy being with my husband, wherever that is."

"So you don't go out on your own, say to a movie or a dinner?"

"Never."

What business is it of yours? The question was on the tip of her tongue, but she kept it there. He was too interested, looked at her too closely, she thought.

"Did you have any other business you wanted to discuss?" she asked.

"Afraid not. I wanted to see you and congratulate you on writing an unbiased story about me...us. The work will go on. We will recruit more and more, just as I said before. Yes, we'll protect, but in doing that we'll need to fight. We know the enemy, and it is our own terrorist government, Jewish bankers and media moguls, and non-white infiltrators. Sometime soon…"

He paused in reflection.

"Sometime soon? What?" Astrid said.

"I'm not here to pontificate. Like I said, I am here to express my admiration for you. It has been a pleasure to see you again, Astrid. Now, I must go along. I have to prepare for an operation."

About to offer regret at hearing that, Astrid stood up. He had more to say.

"You're a fine person, Astrid Lincoln. You've brightened my life. Give my regards to your husband. He's a lucky man. And if that sounds like jealousy, it is. Another time, another place…but timing is everything, isn't it?"

He put on his coat and buttoned it, while Astrid stood speechless. This whole discussion had been bizarre. He moved toward the door and she followed, expecting his quick exit. Instead, he turned and placed his hand on the side of her face. She might have pulled away, but not wanting an ugly finish to this meeting, she waited.

"You have lovely skin, soft and pure, like your soul. Thank you for talking with me, Astrid."

Unhurried, he leaned forward and kissed the corner of her mouth, then left.

Dazed, she remained in front of the door, put her hand over the place he kissed, and mused, "What the hell was that all about?"

CHAPTER 29

She didn't mention the kiss, but when Abram came home at ten and they had their usual coffee and cookies at the kitchen table, Astrid told him about General Metcalf's visit.

"I never expected a thank-you," she said. "I thought he'd blast me for writing scurrilous stuff about his camp. Instead he said it was publicity that he couldn't have bought. Imagine that."

"If that's what he calls publicity, I'd hate to think what it would take to get him mad."

"He said two men have already visited him because of the story. They want to join his group. They feel called upon to fight tyranny. What kind of madness have I created?"

Abram took her hand.

"You haven't created any kind of madness, Sweetheart. General Metcalf has. He's the one recruiting to carry out his treachery. If you think you haven't made the point that this is lawlessness in the long run, then perhaps you should use stronger language in another story, or maybe Charlie should write an editorial denouncing the movement."

"I don't know. Causes usually seem to me like wasted energy. Just look at what a cause has done to Cat. She couldn't stop herself after a while, just had to keep on screaming about how everyone was going to be killed in their beds by these men with guns blazing. I feel that I've gone as far as I can, or want to go, on this whole situation. As long as he doesn't break the law, I'm satisfied that Metcalf isn't doing any harm. After all, it's a small group. His dream of great expansion can't be realized very soon, and he'll become too old to lead a real fight before he knows it."

Abram shrugged.

"You were full of contempt for him and his militia before you wrote the story. What's changed?"

"I don't know. Maybe I saw a different image of him in a regular suit, out of uniform. He could have been any man."

"Except that he still talks like a renegade soldier, I'll bet."

"Ya. That's true. Well, we'll see. For now, I'd like to give it a rest."

What *had* she seen in General Metcalf? A weakness? Compassion that she hadn't seen previously? And why did he make up to her that way? Of all the questions, that one was the most disturbing.

She was clearing the dishes away when Abram said, "Freddy was acting stranger than usual today."

"He sounds like a real character."

"He is that. When I got to the office, he was jumpy and far-away in another world somewhere. I spoke to him, just asked how the family was, and he didn't answer, so I asked again. When he finally looked at me, you'd have thought he'd seen a ghost. He said he guessed everyone was okay. And he added, 'For now, anyway.' I was going to ask what he meant by that, but all of a sudden he just bolted out of the office without saying goodbye. He did say something about he hoped we'd all survive Sunday."

"That *was* odd. Is it a full moon tonight? Everyone seems to have gone a bit berserk."

. . . .

In his motel room, General Metcalf poured himself a Scotch, and sat in a chair, looking out at shadows darting about on moonlit snow. He'd never played golf here, but it looked like a good course, even under snow. As he had for the past two nights, he went over flaws in his plan for Sunday's action. Planning was the secret to success. He had always told his troops they had to plan ahead for a sneak attack. If he didn't want anything to go wrong Sunday, he must be able to act without thinking, just follow a well thought-out route of action, like any war games, but be prepared for the unexpected.

The governor would speak in the auditorium, so everyone would be crowded in to hear him. He still debated whether that was the place to launch an open attack, or whether to station himself in some place across the street where, without being seen, he could pick off the governor and a few others coming out of City Hall. He had no death wish, and an attack inside the building would without doubt result in his own death. It was the only plausible outcome. Still, the anonymity of sniper shooting didn't appeal to him. In all previous visions, he'd been inside.

What if he died doing it? Would Astrid grieve for him? Wouldn't she have just a bit of sympathy and say to herself that General Leo Metcalf was a good man, a real leader, seeking to promote a non-intrusive government? She couldn't deny his commitment to that end. An assassination would make the strongest statement of any. It would prove dedication to cause. And because he would do it alone, to die for what he believed in would prove his bravery. How many would do that?

"When it's over, my dear Astrid, you can write a glowing obituary for me. Tell the public that when I said I would protect them, I meant it. You can call me a hero. In fact, I should write things down about myself. I'll do that. I'll tell her all about my past bravery when I fought for this ungrateful United States. I'll tell her how I was wounded in Viet Nam, but never gave up, how I should have received the Purple Heart, but never did. They questioned my wound. Politics. I'll tell her about that, too. They knew about my bravery, but they said I wasn't eligible. Well, they can shove their eligibility. I'm General Leo Metcalf. I'll show the world."

For the fourth time, he poured a glass of Scotch. His wife wouldn't shed a tear if he died. His son might. His daughter would look at her girl friend and say, "Dad understood."

Who would miss him most? He thought he had three good men at The Kingdom, but like Brutus they abandoned their king in time of need. They wouldn't give a damn.

"No matter. I'll write a letter to you, Astrid. I'll show you how much I cared for you. No one else though. You're my girl. I'll give you a call. I'll tell you."

He lifted the phone. But when a man's voice answered, he slammed down the receiver.

"Don't want to talk with that husband. Doubt he even appreciates her. No one can appreciate her like I do. I could have been her husband. I would have loved her more than anyone can. I'll show you all what a leader I am. How much I care about everyone. And I'll show you, Astrid, how much I love you."

The night wore on and he drank more until the quart was three-fourths empty. He raged and rammed around the room. He opened his door and yelled down the hallway.

"I'm the general. I'll show you all. I'm king. I will rule."

Somehow through his fog, he saw figures coming toward him. He closed the door, went to the bed and flopped on it, face down.

Late the next morning, he came to, sick, thirsty for more to drink.

"Got to get awake. Can't be like this. It won't do. I can't plan if I'm out of it. Must get the plan ready. What day is this? I must be ready by Sunday."

CHAPTER 30

Thursday morning, Astrid did not tell anyone at the office about the general's visit to her home. She rationalized that it wasn't necessary, but somewhere in the reaches of her sub-conscience, she felt a strange guilt that the general had found her attractive and that he made overtures to that effect in her own home. If she said anything about his visit, she might be pressed for a reason that he went there, and with that bit of self-blame scratching at the surface, she might end up telling all. Of course, she reasoned, she wasn't at fault if someone thought she was more than she was, but the only one she wanted to think that was Abram.

Will brought his wife and two children to the office so that they could meet Charlie and Astrid and see where he worked. His daughter Julia and son Travis were the kind of kids Astrid liked--quiet. Travis, like his father, had wavy bleached blond hair and blue eyes while Julia stood apart from both parents, with braces on her buck teeth, straight dark hair with red highlights and dark eyes. She had personality that never stopped even when she stood still.

Astrid warmed to Will's children immediately, and before they left she asked if they'd like to go to the college Saturday for an hour or two of skating at the new hockey rink. She suggested that they could also look around the campus.

Travis said, "Yeah. That's cool."

"Yes!" Julia said in a burst of enthusiasm. "It's okay, isn't it, Mom?"

"Of course," Geena said. "Will?"

"Just be home by five." He looked at Astrid. "I'm taking the family to see *Back To The Future, Two*."

"Well we'll be sure to get you home by five," Astrid said. "You won't want to miss that film."

On Friday, Fairchance residents woke up to another snowstorm, a big one. By noon it had not let up. Astrid had made the last phone call on her list for interviews.

"I'm sure glad Jenny and I got settled here," Charlie said. "I'd hate to drive to Twin Ports in this stuff. Well, I wouldn't, of course. I'd stay at the motel again."

"You and me both," Will said. "I don't know about tomorrow, Astrid. If the roads aren't open, just skip it. The kids will have fun outside, anyway. And we can all walk to the theater."

"Ya. I may have to do that. We'll have a lot of shoveling to do. Will you explain to the kids? Tell them we can do it next week. Or should I call?"

"No need to call. I'll tell them. They'll be okay with it."

"Then I'll plan to take them next Saturday."

Dee came downstairs just before noon and stepped into the office. Astrid noted how alive she had become since accepting Marvin's proposal. Whenever they were together, they looked like a couple of teenagers just venturing into the adult world of love and marriage.

"I hope everyone's going home," Dee said. "This is coming down fast."

"I was about to tell Astrid and Will we wouldn't work this

afternoon," Charlie said. "How're you doing up there all by your-self, Dee?"

"I'm fine by myself. But I won't be alone for long. Nelson will move up from the business office. He'll have the office adjoining mine. We should do very well with the arrangement."

Astrid wasted no time packing it in and leaving for the week-end. She would be on the job Sunday afternoon, and Abram would be working that day beginning at noon, so this would give them a few hours before then to shovel snow and possibly have some fun in the game room. He had painted it red with white trim, a color that Holly said the owners would not object to, since they had given Astrid and Abram permission to do anything they wished, but not make structural changes or in any way change the restoration they had done.

"Hi, I'm home," Astrid called down the basement stairway. "You down there, Abram?"

"Be right up."

She was ravenous, and started making grilled cheese sand-wiches, coffee, and cottage cheese and peach salads.

"We're not working this afternoon," she said when Abram came in. "How's it going down there?'

"Looking good. I can see that you're hungry, so we'll go down and look at it after lunch. Hey. I hadn't looked out the window for a couple of hours. The snow is piling up fast. Too bad we don't have a plow on the front of that Jeep."

He was teasing. They had this conversation a couple times before, and she always rejected the idea of hauling around a snow-plow all winter. Today she thought she'd tease right back.

"Well, maybe you're right," she said. "I hear that it's not much of a job at all to take it off and put it back on. Ya. Maybe we should go get one when we can get out."

He sucked in his cheek for a bit while he hemmed and hawed.

"Well, I guess it won't do us a great deal of good now, will it? Maybe another year we should think of it. Probably won't get much more snow this year. Not much point in horsing around with it just now."

"If you really feel that way. Are you sure?"

"Uh huh. I'm sure."

"Then I'll call Stumpy after we eat and be sure he'll plow us out when the snow stops. He'll be busy."

"Trouble is there isn't much of any place to put the snow any more. We're lucky here with the hillside below us, but the city will be in big trouble."

"I hope the governor can still make it Sunday."

"Roads should be open by then, especially the main roads. You said you're taking Cat."

"Ya. She called me today and wanted to be sure I wouldn't forget. She's funny. When her husband isn't around, she still talks about the gun problem. I wouldn't be at all surprised if she went up to the governor and asked what he plans to do about controlling the sale of guns in the state."

"Has she written any letters lately?"

"Not that I know of. She hasn't said anything about my story this week. I know she still believes all guns should go. If only it were that simple."

Abram helped her by setting the table. When they began to eat, he became quiet. Astrid recognized the sign that he had something on his mind.

"Not the ring, is it?" she said.

"What?"

"You're not thinking about the ring again, are you?"

He laughed.

"No, not the ring. But I am a bit worried that the general might show up at the governor's speech. Did he say anything about that?"

"No. I didn't think to ask, either."

That was unlike her, she thought. Why didn't she probe to find out if he planned a disturbance at City Hall?

"Maybe he didn't stay in town," she said. "Maybe he only came here for some business, or for a health problem. He was dressed in street clothes. And he did say he had to see about an operation. Maybe he's not well."

"Promise me if you see him there you'll get out."

"Abram, you know I can't do that. I'll be working. Besides, there will be a lot of people. I don't think he'd do anything to endanger all of them to get at the governor."

But she remembered only too well his words as she was getting into her Jeep when leaving The Kingdom. *One day you will see the real Patriots in action, when we begin our offensive drive that will start the revolution.*

This couldn't possibly be the time for such a terrible attack. So small a group, such a small army. If he should be planning a revolution, he would have to engage more than his militia. He'd need all those militias that he opined about in their interview, all over the United States. A little group of men in this one Maine county could do nothing. Even the local police could restrain them.

CHAPTER 31

Astrid awoke to bright sunshine streaming through the bedroom side window. She sat up straight in bed, saw that Abram was already gone, and looked at her clock. Nearly nine o'clock. How could she have overslept so long, and why didn't Abram wake her?

He was reading the newspaper when she got to the kitchen, and she saw that he hadn't had breakfast. Places were set and the grill was open beside a bowl that she presumed held the batter for pancakes.

"Why didn't you wake me up, Abram? How long have you been waiting for me?"

"Not long. You needed your beauty sleep."

"You're the one who worked late. You needed as much or more sleep as I did."

He folded the newspaper and put it next to her plate.

"I woke up when Stumpy started to plow."

"Oh? I never heard it myself."

"Not surprising. You do sleep well. Just like a pet pig I used to have when I was a kid."

"A pet pig, huh? Well, you snore like the pig's granddad."

"So you're calling me an old boar?"

"If the shoe fits."

Their jabs were interrupted by the clack sound of the front door mail slot .

"I'll get it," Abram said. "Stumpy's bill, no doubt."

When he returned, he said, "It's the bill. And here's something from the real estate agency. I didn't see it yesterday. Suppose they want us to leave?"

"I hope not. Open it and find out."

He slit the envelope and pulled out a letter.

Still grilling pancakes, Astrid looked over.

"What does it say?"

"Give me a second. Oh. This is interesting. She says the Wilsons have decided not to return here and want to sell this house. She thought she'd give us first refusal on it, since we've been living in it, and hopes she might hear from us one way or the other within a week. She enclosed the listing sheet."

Astrid brought the plate of pancakes to the table without comment.

"Well?" Abram said. "What do you think?"

"I think I'm stunned. I must say I really like the place. It's beautiful and has a wonderful view of the city and beyond."

She picked up the listing sheet.

"Considering the house, the view, the land, I think the price is reasonable. But, of course, I did want the new house. Then, again, you have a full-time job now. I don't know that you would have time to build that new one."

She left the table and brought back the coffee pot.

"What do *you* think, Abram?"

"Don't expect me to make the choice. It's your money, and your decision. I will point out that you have valuable land in the city. What? Two acres? That will sell quickly and at a high price."

"That's true. And I wasn't greatly impressed with that

neighborhood, to tell the truth. You wouldn't be disappointed not to build a house?"

"No way. I can do it, and I enjoy building, but I also like working at the Sheriff's Office. Now is a good time to tell you, I guess. I was talking with Larry a few days ago about the possibility of an advancement after a while. He suggested that I look into a law enforcement study course. When I'm ready, he'll take me on as a deputy."

"A deputy sheriff. You think you'd like that work, Abram?"

"I do. I talk with the deputies a lot. A couple of them come in each night and tell me about their day before they leave for home. Yeah. I'd like to be part of that."

"So you'd have to go away to school."

She regretted the tone of disappointment in her voice. But how could she bear to have him in some other city, or even some other state, studying?

"Not very far. They have the program right here at Fairchance College."

"No kidding. I didn't know that."

Now she smiled. Of course she wouldn't have objected if he had to go away somewhere to get the courses he needed, despite her disappointment, but to have him home while he was studying would be perfect.

"Then let's do it, Abram. Let's buy this house and enroll you in college and get you ready to wear a deputy sheriff's uniform."

"I hope you won't love me just because I look handsome in a uniform."

"In or out of uniform, I'll love you, Honey. I do love you. I'm really happy and proud of you, and happy for our decision to stay right here. This is all very exciting. We have a terrific life ahead. I just know it."

. . . .

Leo Metcalf studied his reflection in the bathroom mirror. He smoothed his hair and studied his mustache. Ten years ago he had begun planning for the moment when he would etch his name at the top of an eternal slate of heroic leaders. Tomorrow, that great moment would happen. He would become immortal in the eyes of Patriots everywhere. His name would be spoken in reverence as a pioneer in the movement leading to the revolution. Others would take up the cause, but no name would go down in history for bravery, for foresight like that of General Leo Metcalf for one simple reason: he led the state of Maine Patriots by staging the state's first meaningful attack on a statesman and his followers. He'd symbolize the meaning of Maine's motto, *Dirigo*.

"I, General Leo Metcalf, will direct. I will be the leader."

Even the men of his militia didn't think he could pull it off, but they were wrong. He would be martyred, and they would be left to work out the route of revolution from there. He had left behind a comprehensive plan for the work to be carried out. If they followed it, they would succeed. But it meant working harder, giving up the luxuries. They'd need to abandon that good life he had given them and live deeper in the woods, moving often, staying out of reach of the law. They already had stashes of weapons and medical supplies that couldn't be found if authorities snooped around The Kingdom after tomorrow. His soldiers should thank him for that foresight, too.

It would be a long night of waiting, but tomorrow would come. Tomorrow, Bloody Sunday in Fairchance.

. . . .

He had slept quite peacefully as it turned out, and Leo felt all the better for a good rest. He faced the day feeling ten feet tall, full of enthusiasm for the task ahead. As a bonus, the day had turned warm, and would reach 25 degrees, according to the weatherman. That would feel like spring. Couldn't be better.

He dressed in full uniform, making sure his medals were in proper order. In checking each one, he lingered over a few of them and chuckled, recalling how he had come by them. They were authentic enough, just hadn't been presented to him personally. But the Army-Navy Store owner let him have them at a price he couldn't resist.

Breakfast in the dining room was complete with eggs, bacon, muffins, coffee. Nothing like a good breakfast before facing a day's work.

On returning to his room, he packed his case, attached a note where it should be sent, watched more news and learned that the governor was on schedule. The network promised live coverage of the governor's tour today, so he would be shown to the world in his hour of glory.

The one case that he would carry was his briefcase, large enough to hold two semi-automatic handguns, as well as extra clips. He'd never get to use them all, but he had no doubt he could get off 30 rounds without interruption, maybe more if only a couple of officers were on duty. After all, they had no forewarning that there might be trouble, so why would they station more? Fairchance would be Littlechance when he opened fire. At that, he laughed aloud.

"That's a good one. Littlechance. Too bad I don't have some way to give that to Astrid. She'd appreciate my humor."

CHAPTER 32

Astrid had kissed Abram goodbye when he left for the beginning of his full-time work as a sheriff's dispatcher, and now she drank her second cup of coffee while reading a Sunday newspaper feature concerning the relatively new discussion of global warming.

When she finished that and cleaned up the kitchen, it was time to begin getting ready to pick up Cat and head for City Hall. It wasn't melting outside, but it looked softer as the temperature began to rise. She looked forward to springtime when she could work in the soil. She thought this year she could plant a small vegetable garden in back of the garages. She would also plant petunias in a round bed out front.

She chose a beige sweater to wear with brown pant suit. As she braided her hair, she wondered once again what Abram would think if she had her hair cut. Though she never was one to think much about style, she had begun to think of this twist of braid as being burdensome when it came to getting herself ready for work each day. She would talk it over with him first. A lot of wives would just do it and surprise their husbands, but she wasn't great on creating surprises that could backfire.

She left the house at 1:30. As soon as she drove up to the

back door, Cat came running out. She had replaced her heavy winter coat and long wool scarf with a pretty green wool coat and matching scarf.

"Lovely day," she said, fumbling for the seat belt.

"Very. How nice you look, Cat. I've never seen you dressed up before."

"Oh, I can. I have a closet full of clothes that I seldom wear any more. Coats are always long on me, but under this I have a peach suit. Roy said I was pushing spring in these colors, but I like it. It does us good to get gussied up once in a while, don't you think?"

"Ya. I agree."

"You always look fresh and pretty," Cat said. "I'd have killed for your height."

Astrid looked down at her and thought what a lively young woman she must have been. Pretty or not, she had the personality that charmed.

As they approached City Hall, Cat began to worry.

"It's crowded. Oh, I do hope none of that militia group comes. I have to tell you I've worried about this meeting. Governor Monohan is popular here. I knew he'd attract a crowd."

Astrid parked and waited for Cat to alight. Together, they walked up the stairs and into the hall where many were milling about. The buzz of chatter kept rising, until someone yelled out that they should all go inside and be seated.

"Wait a minute, Cat," Astrid said. "I want to be at the back of the room. I'll take photos from there. Charlie will be up front."

When everyone had gone in, Astrid and Cat found chairs against the back wall and sat down. It was only a matter of seconds before the governor entered from the other end of the room, stood at the podium, and expressed thanks that so many had come to talk with him. He would hold a question and answer session after he gave his remarks.

"He's so handsome," Cat whispered.

Astrid took pictures using natural light and long lens while the governor talked.

"Not just handsome," Astrid whispered in Cat's ear. "but a good speaker, too."

"Too bad he got married."

"Why Cat. I detect a devilish streak in you."

"I never gave up dreaming."

The governor appeared ready to close his talk, when Astrid looked at a man who entered the room quickly and stood at the back, two chairs beyond Cat. There was something familiar about the man, but at first she didn't recognize him. When he laid his briefcase on an empty chair and unsnapped it, she saw, and recognized.

"Oh my God," she said. "It's General Metcalf."

He had shaved off his mustache, and wore a knit cap over his red hair. A long raincoat covered his clothing.

When she heard the name, Cat looked his way, saw the lid up on his case. She jumped to her feet, opened her purse, took out the gun replica, and pointed it at the general.

"Stop, General Metcalf," she yelled. "Close that case or I'll shoot."

The room began to buzz with questions of what was going on. Everyone turned around to see.

A woman screamed, "She's got a gun!"

When Astrid saw what Cat was doing, she shouted, "No, Cat. Don't."

The speed of the action that followed would always astound Astrid in relating the details.

The general heard Cat's name, and saw the gun in her hand. In one swift move, he took a weapon from his briefcase, held it with both hands and aimed at Cat. Four shots in quick succession rang out…pow, pow, pow, pow. Pandemonium erupted as women and men screamed and shouted. Some tried to crawl under benches, others stood, too horrified to move.

Astrid dropped to her knees and bent over Cat, but she knew the worst. Her friend, bleeding from two head wounds, was dead. Astrid felt a wave of nausea, looked up, and saw the gun pointed at her. Time stood still. She froze and thought, "This is it."

The general's wild eyes focused on her. He stopped. His mouth went slack and his eyes softened.

"Not you, not you," he said, shaking his head.

In the same instant, a barrage of shots rang out. The general collapsed, not in dramatic contortions as in movies, but all at once, falling flat on his back. The gun, still in his hand, was dead, too, a useless tool without an operator. The body and the silent gun held Astrid's attention, until she heard voices around her.

"Someone call an ambulance," a voice cried out.

Uncontrollable shaking took over Astrid's body. She fell backward to a sitting position, wrapped her arms around her knees, laid her head against them, and gasped for breath.

· · · ·

She recalled later that the sheriff appeared at her side and helped her up, asked if she would be all right, did she want him to drive her home. She answered she was okay. She said she thought she should go to the office. She asked that someone cover Cat's body, and the sheriff took off his coat and covered the dead woman

"Where did all of you come from?" she wanted to know.

"I had an informant. He told us he thought this would happen."

Why she went to the office, she could never explain, except

that it seemed like the right thing to do. *Get there. Go to work.* The words ran through her mind, over and over again while she drove.

The office was cold, and she found herself shaking when she began to type. It occurred to her that she should call Abram, in case no one else had.

When they were connected, she heard panic in his voice.

"My God. Are you all right, Astrid? Tell me. Are you okay?"

"Ya. Ya. I'm okay. Stop worrying. I'm okay. It was Cat, you know. She was shot. She saved everyone else."

"I didn't know who. I got the ambulance call. I was frantic to know if you had been shot. But you're okay?"

"Ya. I said I was. General Metcalf. He disguised himself. I didn't know him until he leaned over for his gun. Then I saw. He…he was shot, too. It was so bloody. I've still got blood on my clothes from poor Cat. Where did all those officers come from?"

"Look, dear, I have to go. This place is hopping. Go home and rest. We'll talk when I get there."

"Ya. Okay."

But she didn't go home. She sat and wrote fast, as the details came rushing in and the significance of Cat's act loomed as the most heroic thing she had ever seen, as well as the fact that it was Cat who had cautioned everyone that the militia was dangerous. She was the voice in the wilderness to ban guns. Simply that. Get rid of guns. And yet if a mad man hadn't been intent on an assassination this day, there would have been no shootings. The guns would have remained silent, doing no harm.

"Get rid of the madness," Astrid yelled to the four walls while she typed. She wrote the words as she said them. "It's insanity, crazy thoughts of fighting the status quo by violence. Intolerance and hate. Little men who are afraid of not being heard. Stop the hate! Stop the intolerance."

. . . .

When Abram came through the door, he called Astrid's name. All was quiet. He shouted again. Still no answer. Where was she? Did she tell him the truth? Was she okay or was she shot, too? Maybe she had to go to the hospital.

He took the stairs two at a time and went to their bedroom. There he found her sound asleep. He almost collapsed.

"Astrid? You okay?" he said as quietly as he could but loud enough, he hoped, to wake her.

When she didn't wake up, he gently shook her arm. She roused, opened her eyes, and bolted upright to throw her arms around his neck.

"I'm so glad you're home, Abram. This has been a nightmare. Just a nightmare."

"I know. I know. I'm here now. You want to go downstairs and talk a while? It's only 8:15."

"Ya. Let's talk."

All the way down the stairs, he kept his arm around her, though she seemed steady on her feet. He just couldn't let her go.

Instead of coffee, he made hot chocolate.

"My mother always said this calms a person better than coffee."

"She was right," Astrid said. "How did it go on your end after the shooting?"

"Busy. I was going crazy not knowing if you were shot. All I heard was that there were gunshots, and two people were killed. God, Astrid, I was close to leaving my post and running over to City Hall to see if you were alive."

"I should have had the sheriff tell you, but I couldn't think straight."

"I know what you mean. Did the sheriff tell you that Cat Cotter didn't have a real gun?"

"No, but I knew that. It looked like a real one, but it was a cigarette lighter. Charlie had told me she had pulled it out and scared him and Dee one day. Then she said it was just a cigarette lighter. Oh dear God, Abram He shot her for nothing. She must have known that would happen. She drew his attention to herself rather than let him shoot the governor, you see."

"He didn't get off another round, they said, even though he had 26 rounds left in the Ruger. You were right next to Cat, weren't you? I wonder why he didn't shoot you."

"I really don't know. He pointed the gun at me, I know. But for some reason he lowered the gun, and then came all those shots. He flopped backward and never moved a muscle."

Astrid fought the tears, thinking of Cat, lifeless on the floor. The poor woman, killed by a gun, the very thing she had been fighting against all these years. She finally got everyone's attention. Would it do any good?

"They said if he hadn't hesitated, just that few seconds," Abram said, "he would have snuffed out several lives, and most likely that of the governor. Just that few seconds."

It was all he could say. If it hadn't been for those few seconds, he'd have lost Astrid.

They stayed in the kitchen, sometimes talking, sometimes just sitting and mulling over the horrible events in silence, for another hour before deciding to go to bed. Before Abram turned out the light for the night, he looked over at his wife, almost overcome with the realization that he might have been going to bed alone tonight.

"I have to tell you something, Honey," he said.

"What is it?"

"After I got the first call about the shooting, I began saying, 'That damned ring.'"

Astrid's laugh was almost hysterical. "You know what? I said it a few times, too."

CHAPTER 33

The following Sunday morning, just as he had promised by phone earlier in the week, Gunnar came to visit. He made no pretense of indifference, but held Astrid in a firm embrace.

"That was too close a shave, Sister. Don't scare us all like that again, huh?"

"Not if I can help it, you can be sure."

"Hey, brother-in-law," he said to Abram, "how're you holding up?"

"We're all getting back to normal, as much as we ever will."

They chose the cozy book-lined den for coffee and talk. Gunnar noticed that his sister was very quiet, not typical of her. Abram looked untouched by the tragedy, but there was no doubt that Astrid would take a while to get there.

"How is Charlotte?" Abram asked.

"She's getting big. But she's quite happy at the prospect of motherhood."

"And you?" Astrid said. "Are you happy now that you're over the wanderlust and settled on the business?"

"Ya. It's good. You were right, though. I did need help, and thanks. I have some good workers now, so I spend most of my time at my desk. A lot of paper work to do."

After small talk, Gunnar got around to asking about the shooting.

"That was a close call for the governor, Astrid. And for you, I gather. That general was the one you'd written about running a militia in the woods?"

"Ya. General Metcalf. I'm afraid his big ideas about expanding into an international organization, with himself as the commander, ended right then and there."

"Not only that," Abram added, "but the men and women who were at that compound of his, living in luxury from what I've been told, have all disbanded and gone away somewhere. The sheriff told me they think everyone quickly got out of there before the FBI could arrive. He thought they might be headed for a southern state where they may join up with similar groups. But with that town they built at The Kingdom, it's likely they'll return. They'll be watched closely, of course."

Gunnar closed his eyes.

"You look tired," Astrid said. "You aren't sleeping?"

"More or less. Charlotte is restless, keeps me from sleeping sometimes. I was just thinking about a little band of wannabe soldiers here in Maine. Unbelievable."

"They weren't as invisible as everyone thought," Abram said. "The sheriff had a pretty good handle on what they were up to, most of the time."

Astrid turned to Abram.

"You seem to have gotten a lot of information about all of this, Dear."

"To tell the truth," he said, "there's something I didn't tell you. You remember when I said Freddy was acting more fidgety than usual one night before the shooting?"

"Ya."

"It seems that Freddy was sort of a double agent, funny as that sounds here in Maine. He was working for the general as a spy of sorts, and at the same time he was reporting their activities to the sheriff. When he heard the general's plan for doing harm to the governor, he wasn't sure what to do that night, because he didn't want to create an incident when there might not be one. In the end, he went to Larry and told him all about the way the general had been acting more crazy than usual, and that he was quite sure he would stage an assault on the governor."

"When did you find out about all this?" Astrid said.

"Not until Wednesday. Freddy came in to tell me he was moving away with his family. Said he was taking a similar position in Rhode Island. It was then that he gave me the scoop on all that he'd been up to. Anyway, he was glad that he finally went to Larry with his concerns. He also said the other militia men wouldn't join the general. Since they didn't know what Metcalf would do, the sheriff had City Hall swept for a possible bomb Sunday morning, and he had State Police there as well as the local lawmen."

"But I never saw them. They just appeared out of nowhere."

"Most of them were in plain clothes, not to make people nervous."

Astrid stood up and went to the red brick fireplace to warm her hands.

"So that's why there were so many shots."

"That's why. I didn't tell you the night I found out about it because you had seemed a little depressed, and I didn't want to open it all up again."

Gunnar had listened with interest.

"I don't know if I can ever get used to the lives you two lead. You're a regular sleuthing couple, like Nick and Nora North. You know, you really ought to start a private investigation business. You could call it something like 'A.A. Lincoln, Honest Investigations.' What do you think?"

"Oh Gunnar," Astrid said. "That's ridiculous. Since when did a small city like Fairchance need a couple of private investigators? Just plain silly."

"Well, now, I don't know, Dear." Abram said, with a wink at Gunnar. "You have a particular flair, a nose for trouble. You were on the trail of bank robbers in Florida, remember."

Gunnar slid forward in his chair.

"Really? What's that all about?"

"Abram. Don't you dare tell him about that."

Ignoring her command, Abram said, "It seems that the hotel where we stayed was across the street from a bank, and one day Astrid saw suspicious activity going on."

"Abram!"

"Ya, go on," Gunnar urged.

"Two men who were supposed to be playing chess in the lobby of our hotel were just moving pieces about, and, quick of eye and wit, Astrid figured that they were casing the bank. Then when they ran out and got some guns..."

"They were handed guns by men who drove up in a car," Astrid said. "What was I to think?"

"Certainly," Gunnar said.

"She ran back and forth like a chicken with its head cut off, telling the desk clerk to call the police. The men who went into the bank all came out and drove away. Now, Astrid was about out of her mind when the police did come. She shot across the street--despite my advice to stay out of it."

Gunnar was already getting the picture and stifling a laugh.

"I could see the policeman talking with her, and instead of coming back to the hotel like he told her to, she pulled him from the police car, and..."

"I did not pull him. I simply touched his arm and asked him to listen to me."

"Like I said, she pulled him from the car and held him in place while she told him about those dangerous men. Finally, when she got back, she looked like a cat that lost a mouse down a hole--you know, all indignant as if to say 'I didn't want it anyway.'"

"Well, what was it all about? Was there a bank robbery?"

"No. The men she called robbers were also police officers. They were stationed there to be sure there wouldn't be a robbery since there was a large cash deposit being made by the men in the car. And Astrid nearly got ticketed for assaulting an officer."

"Oh." Gunnar and Abram both burst into riotous laughter that went on for a full two minutes. Finally, Astrid laughed, too.

"Well, you have to admit," she said, "it looked like a robbery in progress."

"And then you came home after only a week," Gunnar said. "Is that why?"

"Oh no," Astrid said. "The weather was unbelievably cold. We found out that people coming back from their cruise couldn't enjoy beaches or tours at ports of call, so we gave it up and went back to the hotel. So when Charlie called and said they needed me back here, we were ready to do it. And then I was assigned to interview General Metcalf."

"The woman who was killed," Gunnar said, "how was she involved?"

"She was the one who brought the group to our attention. She had been fighting for gun controls for many years, after her brother was shot in a drive-by shooting on a street in Boston."

"Why did the general shoot only her?"

"She took a gun from her purse and pointed it at him. Only it was not a gun, just a cigarette lighter that looked authentic. She did it to draw his attention to herself. Otherwise, the governor would have been dead before the lawmen could get the general."

It occurred to Astrid that all of that was in her story.

"Didn't you read my story this week, Gunnar?"

"No. I didn't get it. I think someone around there is taking my paper. This is the third week in a row that I didn't get it."

"I'll give you one before you leave."

Abram said, "Something else we want to give you, Gunnar."

He raised an eyebrow at Astrid.

"Oh yes," she said. "Gunnar, I want you to know that we both think you were terribly thoughtful to provide a beautiful ring for Abram to give me at our wedding."

"I can guess what's coming," Gunnar said.

"Well, Abram and I went to the jewelry shop, and we bought matching wedding rings."

She went to Abram and they held out their left hands, showing off the rings.

"How about that," Gunnar said. "Platinum with diamonds?"

"That's right," Abram said. "Your aunt's ring is way and above anything else, but we decided that it would be nice to have rings that match. So," he opened a drawer in the stand beside him and took out the velvet box, "we're returning this to you."

"I hope you won't be offended," Astrid said.

"No way. I thought you might do this. A few too many ugly things happen, did they? You fell under the spell of Aunt Alva's curse?"

"Not at all," Abram said. "Anything that happened to us would have happened anyway. Didn't have a thing to do with the ring. I never believed that nonsense about a curse. Never. Not for a second."

(And that was a lie, of course.)

235

NOTES

Numbers of Patriot militia groups, fearful that the federal government was a threat to freedom, were already increasing in the U.S. by 1990.

The Turner Diaries was a real novel by one-time college Professor William Pierce, writing as Andrew Macdonald. The so-called diaries described step-by-step movements of underground bigots determined to annihilate, in the author's words, "Afro-Americans, feminists, gays and lesbians, liberals, communists, Mexicans, democrats, the FBI egalitarians, and Jews." Further, he said, "Especially Jews: for (the book) portrays them as incarnations of everything that is evil and destructive." The FBI reported that Timothy McVeigh's bible was *The Turner Diaries*, containing the blueprint for bombing a federal building. The book became an underground bestseller.

In the mid-1990s Patriot groups numbered some 860. However, by the year 2000, that number had diminished to fewer than 200. Reports indicate that many militia members became disillusioned waiting for a revolution that did not happen and gave it up.

Today, the various Patriot and other hate groups have increased once again. One report listed approximately 1360 hate groups in 2012, up from 200 twelve years previously.

The FBI divides domestic extremists into four broad categories: left-wing, right-wing, single-issue groups, and homegrown Islamic.

The lone offender phenomenon spans all categories. Lone offenders may pose the most immediate threat in the United States. Timothy McVeigh, working with Terry Nichols, is an example. The 1995 bombing of the federal building in Oklahoma City killed 168 persons. Since 1995, the percentage of attacks by individuals acting alone has increased about 25 percent. FBI and police admit that defending against loner attacks is an overwhelming task.

Terrorists often focus on single issues, including environmental degradation, abortion, genetic engineering, animal abuse. Since 1979, some 2000 crimes amounting to $110 million in losses have been committed by one group alone, the Earth Liberation Front. Anti-abortion extremists' acts have resulted in seven murders, 41 bombings, and 173 acts of arson in the U.S. and Canada since 1977.

A lone terrorist in the small city of Belfast, Maine was preparing to create a dirty bomb, and to take it to Washington hidden in the undercarriage of his motor home for the purpose of assassinating President Obama. The man, James Cummings, was shot and killed by his wife December 9, 2008, and she was subsequently spared a prison sentence when evidence of her torment at his hands over the years became evident. Police reported that a big swastika flag hung in their living room and that there were several photographs of Cummings posed in a black Gestapo trench coat. Most of his radioactive materials were purchased through the mail.